Rob emerged from a cabin, shading his eyes from the glare of the sun.

He put on sunglasses and strode toward her. He'd be... good-looking in college, ... the determined ... ...ly ... the gr... ...em, was no longer a boy. Fa... ... ...ident... A... man.

Sh... ...e him ... ... they w... behind his ... ... she felt them o... her, wh... ... ...en he looked at he... The s... ...ng girl ... d b... or...

Sh... took a deep breath, endeavoring to quiet he... ...y heart. *Get a grip, girl. You're not a star-... eighteen-year-old anymore.* She flashed him a bright smile as he came to a halt before her. "Now where's ... g... i yo... ...d about?"

He abruptly turned and set off on the trail to the log structure, leaving her to trot along behind. It was apparent he didn't plan to make their so-called reunion anything more than superficial.

The Rob of her d...

What's happened t...

Books by Glynna Kaye

Love Inspired

Dreaming of Home
Second Chance Courtship
At Home in His Heart
High Country Hearts

GLYNNA KAYE

treasures memories of growing up in small midwestern towns—in Iowa, Missouri, Illinois—and vacations spent in another rural community with the Texan side of the family. She traces her love of storytelling to the many times a houseful of great-aunts and -uncles gathered with her grandma to share hours of what they called "windjammers"—candid, heartwarming, poignant and often humorous tales of their youth and young adulthood.

Glynna now lives in Arizona, and when she isn't writing she's gardening and enjoying photography and the great outdoors.

High Country Hearts
Glynna Kaye

Love Inspired

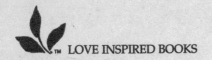

LOVE INSPIRED BOOKS

Recycling programs
for this product may
not exist in your area.

ISBN-13: 978-0-373-81610-1

HIGH COUNTRY HEARTS

Copyright © 2012 by Glynna Kaye Sirpless

www.LoveInspiredBooks.com

Printed in U.S.A.

But God demonstrates his own love for us in this:
While we were still sinners, Christ died for us.
—*Romans* 5:8

Never will I leave you; never will I forsake you.
—*Hebrews* 13:5

To my cousin, friend and published author,
Kathleen Bacus. We've come a long way
from writing and performing plays
in Grandma Belle's basement.

Chapter One

The last time she saw Rob McGuire, he was down on one knee in front of all their friends, diamond ring in hand, and gazing up in hopeful expectation— *at her college roommate*. So what on earth was he doing seven years later on her parents' doorstep? And with a cop no less.

With a quick intake of breath, Olivia Diaz stared from one man to the other, finding Rob's frowning demeanor more encouraging than that of the solemn-eyed officer of the law. But she focused on the latter.

"What's wrong?" Had something happened to her parents? She'd arrived in Canyon Springs shortly after midnight—Tuesday before Labor Day weekend—to an empty house. And now at 7:00 a.m., she'd thought it still too early to call any of her sisters to find out where their folks might be.

"And you are—?" The stocky Native American

officer presented a polite smile, a light breeze ruffling his hair.

"Olivia Diaz." She motioned to the rugged, ponderosa-pine-studded acreage encompassing the rental cabin property her family had run for decades in the high country of Arizona. "My parents—Paul and Rosa Diaz—own Singing Rock."

She shot an anxious glance at Rob, then stepped out the door and onto the front porch of the two-story log home. It *was* Rob, wasn't it? She'd only gotten a few hours of sleep, but surely she wasn't hallucinating. The same trim build, broad shoulders and square jaw. Something in the expressive gray eyes flickered. Did he remember her?

The officer held out identification, again drawing her attention. "I'm Deputy Nate Karel of the County Sheriff's Department, here to see Mr. or Mrs. Diaz. Mr. McGuire here indicated they were out of town, but when we saw signs of habitation at the house, we thought they might have returned."

Tension drained. Her parents were okay.

"No, they're not at home, but in their absence you can speak with me." They'd probably gone on an overnight trip to the Valley of the Sun—the Phoenix area—but she herself would be managing the property in the not-too-distant future. That was her parents' hope, anyway—or had been. After last year's episode it might take some convincing, but she was determined to win them over.

"There's been vandalism to the property." The soft, Navajo cadence of the officer's tone thrummed gently in her ears as he produced a small notebook and pen.

She glanced again at Rob, who seemed to be following the conversation with almost proprietary interest.

What was he doing here?

"And you arrived when, Ms. Diaz?"

Refocusing on the officer, she cringed inwardly, belatedly self-conscious of her bare feet, cut-off shorts and battered Phoenix Suns tank top. Appropriate late-August attire for hanging around the house, but not for hosting a visit from law enforcement—or the man who'd populated her dreams for more years than she cared to admit.

"I got in not long after midnight. Drove all the way from Mississippi to surprise my folks."

Some surprise. No one home. Nothing edible in the fridge. Not even their aging pooch, Maverick, had been around to offer a tail wag.

The officer nodded, seeming to weigh her response as he jotted down a few words. "Did you hear or see anything out of the ordinary at that hour?"

"Such as?"

"Vehicles. Voices. Lights." Amazingly, Rob's mellow tone still sounded familiar to her ears despite the passage of time. "Someone broke into one of the cabins and trashed it."

Great. He appeared out of nowhere in the middle of her world and this was the welcome he got. "Your cabin?"

Rob shook his head. "A vacant one. Timberline."

Then what business was this of his?

"Ms. Diaz?" The deputy drew her attention again. "Would you like to take a look at it? Tell us if anything is missing?"

Like she'd know? She hadn't been out to Timberline in almost a year. To any of the cabins on the property for that matter. Her most vivid memory of the farthest cabin to the west wasn't of its furniture and fixtures, but of a heated argument she'd had there with her oldest sister, Paulette.

"I wouldn't be much help. I've been out of town for quite a while." Besides, much to her shame, now that she knew her folks had come to no harm, her mind wasn't on the issue at hand. Exhilaration bubbled below the surface as she again caught the eye of her old college crush, dressed this morning in a navy blue T-shirt, jeans and charcoal windbreaker. Her heart sped up a notch as he returned her openly curious gaze. He'd always been an eye-catcher, but who'd have thought that was a mere fledgling phase?

"Okay, then," the deputy concluded. "I guess that finishes things up here. I'll file the report, Mr. McGuire. Ms. Diaz. Thank you both for your time."

He shook hands with Rob, nodded at her, then

headed down the steps and toward an official-looking SUV parked in the pine-rimmed clearing.

"Wait." She moved to the edge of the porch, wrapping an arm around one of the thick, hand-hewn wooden posts. If she was to be Singing Rock's manager, she'd better start acting the part. "Do you have any leads? Evidence? Anything forensic to identify the culprits?"

Officer Karel turned. "No, miss, nothing to speak of."

"You'll keep me posted if something comes up?"

"I will. Good day to you both."

She remained standing on the broad wooden porch of the house, watching the officer climb into his county vehicle. An approaching older model minivan passed him on his way out before pulling up in front of another two-story log structure across the clearing—the lodge, hub of Singing Rock activity housing the office, recreation room and an apartment upstairs. Olivia's nose curled at the odor of the vehicle's exhaust, entirely out of place in the pristine, pine-scented retreat. Guests must be returning from an early breakfast or errand run to town.

She turned again to the man standing a few feet away, keeping her arm looped around the post for fear she might float off in euphoria. Drinking in the sight of him, she couldn't disguise the delight in her voice.

"Rob McGuire, of all people. I can't believe after

all this time you've shown up in Canyon Springs. Welcome to Singing Rock."

"Thanks." He brushed an unruly lock of sun-streaked brown hair from his forehead and offered a faint, though not unfriendly smile. But from the puzzlement reflected in his eyes, it was apparent that while he'd heard her name he still hadn't placed her.

"Remember me? Northern Arizona University? Church volleyball team? Friday night Bible study?"

He frowned, uncertainty still evident as he searched her features.

"The sole girl to jump off that bridge during the spring break mission trip to Mexico?" Surely he'd remember that. "The one who came as a smiley face to the church's autumn college kick-off party?"

It was at the costume party where they'd first met and she certainly hadn't forgotten *him*. A debonair masked Zorro. She still remembered his first words to her. *Well, now, aren't you enough to make a man smile.*

Was that romantic or what?

His eyes widened ever so slightly. "It's coming to me now. You dressed all in black and painted your face bright yellow with big black eyes and an ear-to-ear grin."

"Bingo!" *Ha ha.* She'd been stuck the entire evening in that perpetual state long after the other partygoers—including Rob—disposed of removable masks. But freshmen are entitled to a few missteps.

"Well, what do you know? Good to see you again."
Was it?

He continued to study her as if sifting through a box of memories, comparing then and now. "You'll have to forgive me—I thought you looked vaguely familiar when you came to the door, but I sure didn't recognize you."

Thank goodness. Vanity hoped she'd changed since her freshman days of tomboyishly cropped curls, skinny bod and multi-pierced ears. Late bloomer. She proudly shook back her now-cascading black locks, her smile widening in hopes she could coax one from him.

"I still can't believe this. What a small world. I mean, I haven't seen you since—since—"

Their gazes collided at the mutual memory, and from the discomfiture in his eyes she knew he'd remembered her at last. Warmth crept into her cheeks.

Oh, good going, Olivia.

The last thing she wanted to do was remind him of that public turndown of a marriage proposal she and half the church witnessed. Standing but a few feet from the ring's intended recipient, she'd had a front-row seat to his humiliation. "So what brings you here as a guest at Singing Rock?"

With his hands jammed in his jacket pockets, she couldn't get an answer to the question she most wanted to know. Then again, seven years had passed so of course he was married. Guys like him always were. And likely to a woman far more beautiful and spiritual than she'd ever hope to be.

Just her luck, he was probably here with the little wifey and a carload of kids. Or on his honeymoon.

"Actually...I'm the manager here."

Her smile faltered. "Here? At Singing Rock?"

He nodded. "Have been for a couple of weeks now."

She gave an uncertain laugh. No way. As achievement-oriented as Rob had been in college, he had to be heading up his own Fortune 500 company by now. Or maybe even pastoring one of those mega churches. "You're kidding, right?"

He shook his head, his eyes narrowing—apparently at the disbelieving tone of her voice.

Realization slammed into her, leaving a meteor-size crater somewhere in the vicinity of her stomach. Mom and Dad had finally given up on her? They'd hired someone outside the family to run their business?

Her grip tightened on the post as she willed herself to renew a smile. Hiring Rob had to be a temporary situation, right? Until she came back. Until they could get things worked out between them.

"Hey, Rob!" A familiar female voice rang out from across the parking lot where the minivan had pulled up moments ago. She caught sight of her sister Paulette Alston standing beside it. "Would you give me a hand, please?"

Still shaken by Rob's revelation, Olivia stepped back inside the door to retrieve her flip-flops, then caught up with him at what must be her sister's new mom-mobile. She hadn't recognized it when it drove in. A slightly newer model than the last.

Paulette, not expecting to see her this morning, shot Olivia a sharp look as she approached. But Olivia shouldn't have been so surprised to see her oldest sister this early in the day. When you have five kids aged six to sixteen, you have to stay on your toes. This morning Paulette, her senior by a decade, appeared older than her thirty-five years. Black-brown eyes, devoid of the characteristic Diaz sparkle, were shadowed below with dark circles. Tendrils of limp, shoulder-length black hair, haphazardly tied back, escaped to brush her cheeks.

Paulette slid open the side door to the van, gaze focusing on Rob. "What was the deputy doing here? More trouble?"

"Timberline this time."

The hairs prickled along Olivia's arms. "This isn't the first time something like this has happened?"

Her sister shook her head. "Twice now in the past week. Lucky Rob."

Singing Rock's manager fished around in his jacket pocket. As he produced a piece of paper, Olivia at last confirmed the left hand holding it out was ringless. Her heart took flight, but only momentarily. With the way her love life had been going lately, that omission didn't mean much. But ever the optimist, Olivia pounced on the possibility.

"I jotted down a few things while the deputy and I inspected it." Rob unfolded his notes. "They outdid themselves this time."

Olivia stepped closer to get a better look at his neat, compact handwriting, her proximity bringing a fading bruise and healing scrape along the side of his cheekbone into view. Paulette's stare darkened, as if to remind her that by her own choice she had no part in Singing Rock business. Her choice? Not hardly.

"I assume you've introduced yourself to our new manager, Liv?" Dark eyes flashed in obvious satisfaction. She'd never believed her little sister could handle the job and hadn't been afraid to say so.

"Actually, we already know each other." Olivia couldn't help but gloat inwardly as she served up the unexpected spin and watched her sister's smug smile dissolve.

"Oh, really?" Her eyes flitted from Olivia to Rob and back again, her mouth a grim line. "How's that?"

"College," Olivia and Rob said in unison.

Olivia could tell by the arch of Paulette's brow and the look she again darted at Rob that the disclosure met with disapproval. Then again, not much involving Olivia won Paulette's endorsement.

"Small world." Rob's words echoed her earlier

comment, but without the enthusiasm Olivia couldn't help but hope for.

Paulette managed a smile as she turned to Rob and motioned to the interior of her van. "I was in Phoenix over the weekend and picked up supplies at the wholesale warehouse. Would you mind carrying them in for me?"

"I'd be more than happy to." Rob lifted out a box, then headed toward the lodge.

Olivia couldn't help letting her eyes linger on his retreating form. But, not surprisingly, as soon as he was out of earshot Paulette turned to her, blocking the view. "Surprised to see you back, Liv."

"Got in last night." She glanced toward the house, not up to a lecture this morning. "Where are Mom and Dad?"

"They borrowed an RV and headed for Tahoe until October. Left a week ago. You just missed them."

Olivia gasped. "You're kidding. They left town for over a month and didn't even tell me?"

Paulette raised a skeptical brow. "Mom specifically said she emailed you. I hardly think she'd make that up."

"I never got it." Her mind raced to confirm her denial. Things had been so crazy the past few weeks, what with her latest love life derailment and job upheaval. "She should have called me. At least left a message. I can't believe they'd take off before the season's over."

"That's something they can do now that they have a competent overseer of the property. And don't you dare call them about the vandalism and ruin their time off." Paulette glanced toward Rob, returning for another box. As if coming to a decision, she reached into the van, pulled out a couple of jumbo packages of paper towels and thrust them at Olivia. "I told Mom I'd pick up a few things for her, too. Take these to the house, will you? I'll bring the rest in a few minutes when Rob and I are finished with our business."

She could take a hint.

"Good to see you again, Rob." Olivia flashed him a smile as she adjusted the armload of cushiony, tubed cylinders. "Looks as if we'll be seeing quite a bit of each other in the coming days. It'll give us a chance to revisit our NAU memories."

Rob again stuffed his hands in the windbreaker's pockets. Cleared his throat.

Was that a scowl?

"Please don't take this the wrong way, Olivia." His tone held a subtle edge that caught her by surprise. "But reminiscing isn't high on my to-do list. With all there is to take care of around here, I have more than enough to keep me occupied in the here and now."

Just what he didn't need. A shadow from his past. One with big, sparkling brown eyes looking at him like he walked on water. Or at least she had until he

told her he was the new manager of Singing Rock—
and squelched her overture to rekindle their college
acquaintance.

What are you thinking, Lord, bringing me here?

A too-familiar tension gripping his shoulders, he
broke eye contact with her and turned to grab another box. Hefting it into his arms, he strode toward
the lodge, gravel crunching under his work boots.

His grip strengthened on the box as he negotiated
the wide-planked porch stairs, and pulled open the
mullioned door. He'd thought Canyon Springs was
an answered prayer. A haven. A fresh start. But it
now looked like what his grandma called "out of the
frying pan and into the fire."

Crossing the expanse of the somewhat overstuffed
main room, he passed by the staircase that led up to
his quarters and carried the box into the storage room
at the back of the building.

The tension in his shoulders crept down into his
upper arms as he opened the box and shelved the
containers, the shame he could never escape still
washing through him as steadily as a tide since the
moment he'd realized who Olivia was. This couldn't
be happening. Not when things were looking prom-
ising for a change. Not when he'd finally stopped
trying to justify what happened and had thrown himself at God's feet. Begged His forgiveness.

And this was his reward?

Why would God lead him right into home territory

of the president of his college "fan club"—the club he wasn't supposed to know anything about? He'd thought its existence funny back then, in a somewhat embarrassing way. He'd taken a lot of ribbing from the other guys at the church, what with the girls trying to catch his graduate-student eye. Homebaked cookies on his doorstep. Cards and gifts in his mailbox. How many inspirationally-worded bookmarks, plaques and key chains did a guy need?

Yeah, it was flattering back then. Ego-stroking. Amusing at times.

But it was none of the above now.

He shoved the last of the containers onto the shelf and turned to the box he'd brought in first. Sliced it open. Emptied its contents.

What was he going to do?

He couldn't pack up and walk out, leaving Paul and Rosa in a lurch. They were depending on him. They'd given him a vote of confidence early in the game by heading out for rest and relaxation before the mountain country summer visitor season was even over. He couldn't afford to let them down now.

Olivia said they'd be seeing each other in the coming days. How many days? Maybe she wouldn't stay long, be here only for the holiday weekend. He could deal with that, right? Could easily manage to avoid her. He hadn't been joking when he'd said he had more than enough to do around here. He planned to have this place running noticeably smoother by

the time his employers returned and to have the re-
quested development plan mapped out for their approval. He had a lot riding on this job. Everything,
in fact. And not much over a month to prove himself
indispensable, make it permanent.

Olivia obviously thought her parents would be
here. Had a job to get back to—Mississippi, was it?
His heart rate slowed as he clutched at that scrap of
hope.

Regardless of whether or not she was a shadow
from his past, he couldn't afford to get distracted
by a woman like her. Petite, with curves tucked into
figure-skimming denim shorts, her glossy black hair
tumbling around her shoulders to frame the warm
Hispanic skin tones of a delicate face. Brown eyes
danced with mischief.

Carefree and captivating. Exactly like Cassie.

He took a ragged breath.

If there was one thing he knew about a woman
who came packaged like Olivia Diaz, it was that
she'd be a diversion he couldn't afford to indulge in.

Never again.

Chapter Two

❧

Don't take this the wrong way?

"Well, Mr. Robert Thomas McGuire," Olivia mouthed aloud as she dug in the pantry for something to call breakfast, "how else am I supposed to take it?"

She hadn't missed her sister's smirk when he delivered that put-down, either. Where was she, anyway? Twenty minutes later, the minivan was still outside. Surely she wouldn't miss an opportunity to further interrogate her little sister on her out-of-the-blue appearance in Canyon Springs.

But no way was she talking about *that* with Paulette. Maybe with one of her other sisters. Maybe.

She pulled out a cardboard canister of instant oatmeal and stared at the label. Milk or water required. She preferred milk. Looked like she'd be making a run to the grocery store today. With a sigh, she returned the canister to the shelf.

What was it with Rob, anyway? It wasn't *her* fault she'd been front and center when Gretchen dumped him at the church's commencement reception those many years ago. For crying out loud, what kind of dope proposes in front of a roomful of people unless he's one-hundred-percent sure—and then some—that the answer will be Y-E-S? But maybe, like her, he'd never dreamed any woman in her right mind would turn him down.

Of course, it wasn't as if Gretchen hadn't cranked up the charm to grab his attention from the moment Olivia introduced them, so why would he have thought otherwise?

Maybe he blamed her for that, too?

She closed the pantry door harder than intended. Gave it a soft kick for good measure.

"Take it easy, Liv." Paulette's voice intruded into her thoughts as she swept into the kitchen to plunk a box of assorted staples on the table, her handbag skidding across the surface where she'd tossed it. Then folding her arms, she leaned against the work island and—not unexpectedly—got right down to business.

"So, if you and Rob knew each other in college, why don't I remember hearing you talk about him?"

Olivia moved to the table to inspect the box's contents, determined not to let her sister fluster her.

"No reason to, I guess."

Even back then she knew better than to bare her

soul to her sister's scrutiny. She removed two containers of peanut butter from the box and deposited them in the pantry.

"You expect me to believe that?" The tone of Paulette's query was reminiscent of the probing Olivia recalled from her childhood. Big sister who acted more like her mother than her mother did.

She shrugged. "We didn't know each other that well."

"I got the impression from that exchange that there are coals still smoldering. He made it clear he's not into digging up old bones."

"Actually," Olivia speculated, determined to put a positive twist on his response to their reunion, "it sounded to me as if he's overwhelmed with Singing Rock management at the moment. No time to spare."

Paulette's expression clearly stated she wasn't buying it. "You were in classes together? He's older than you, isn't he?"

"He was a grad student my freshman year and helping with the church's college outreach program. We played together on their co-ed volleyball team that winter, Bible study, mission trips, things like that. I didn't even cross his radar."

Sad, but true.

"That's it?" Paulette's tone still echoed disbelief. "No ill-fated fling with you dumping and running?"

"Sorry to disappoint you," she said with a clear conscience as she continued to unpack the box. "So how'd he end up as Singing Rock's manager? He put himself through school working for a property management business, but I didn't think that was his ultimate goal. And certainly not in a dinky town like this."

Paulette shifted her weight. "You missed the wedding last spring, but he's our cousin Joe's new in-law. His wife, Meg's, brother. Guess he recently had a run-in with armed drug dealers in Vegas. A close call."

Olivia winced. Did that account for the bruises and scrapes? "That's scary."

"He hightailed it out of the city, looking for an out-of-the-way place to land. Can't get much more out of the way than Canyon Springs. Joe says he doesn't like to talk about the incident, so don't say anything to him, okay? Don't want him to think people are gossiping about him."

"I won't." But a good-looking single man, new to town, would be bound to stir up talk. Speculation. "This is temporary, right? He's not a permanent manager."

"If he works out—and I think he will—he's exactly what Mom and Dad need. An answered prayer."

Olivia set the pickle jar on the table. "You can determine that this early? He's barely been here a couple of weeks."

"That's longer than you stayed the last time."

Gut-punched, Olivia forced a smile, unwilling to let her sister drag her into a war of words. Again.

"Mom and Dad like him?"

"You think they'd be gadding about this time of year if they didn't? I admit he's on the uptight side. But once the rawness of that Vegas encounter wears off, I imagine he'll fit in here fine."

Uptight might describe him now if his earlier, curt remark could be used as evidence, but that wasn't an accurate description of the Rob she knew in college. Her memory flashed to a long-cherished image of him. His eyes closed. Humming softly. Fingering the strings of his guitar as light from a campfire played across his features.

"He certainly was motivated, ambitious, but never uptight."

"People change, I guess." Paulette glanced at her watch, then snatched her purse from the table. "Gotta go. Have to be at work by eight-fifteen."

"You're working now? Outside the home?" Her sister had always been adamant about being there for the kids. Vowed they'd live off beans and soup until her offspring graduated if that's what it took to be a full-time mother and homemaker.

Paulette scowled, her tone defensive. "The kids are in public school now."

"I didn't mean—"

"Wyatt's Grocery. Clerking."

"Busy place," she commiserated, hoping to establish common ground with her too-sensitive big sis. She remembered her own demanding high school schedule at the local grocer's bakery and deli departments. "On your feet all day."

Paulette grimaced and turned away toward the living room as if she'd already shared more than she'd intended. "So, how long are you staying this time?"

Too long to suit her sister, no doubt. Mom and Dad were understanding when she popped in and out of town. Not Paulette. And maybe not Mom and Dad if hiring Rob was any indication. She couldn't blame them for that. After all, hadn't she herself told them—after her oldest sister pummeled her self-confidence—that it wouldn't work out?

"I don't know," she said, following her sibling to the adjoining room. It had been so clear on the drive home that she'd given up too easily last year, hadn't stood her ground. But with her parents turning to a stranger to fill the Singing Rock management role...

"One word of advice." Paulette jerked open the front door and stepped onto the shaded porch. Her hand still on the doorknob, she turned with an uncompromising glare. "I don't know what you think you're doing coming back here right now, but don't go getting any ideas about Rob McGuire."

"Excuse me?"

"You know what I'm talking about. He can't be another notch on your love life gun belt. The future of Singing Rock is riding on him and you can't come bounding in here with your typical puppy-dog enthusiasm, straining a working relationship with Mom and Dad's new manager. I think you owe them that."

Her sister pulled the door firmly shut behind her.

Olivia stood riveted to the floor. Her love life gun belt? Puppy-dog enthusiasm? And what did she mean the future of Singing Rock was riding on Rob? Just because Mom and Dad were eager to retire and none of their daughters or sons-in-law had an interest in carrying the torch of the family business? That may have been true at one point. But not now. Not after she'd regained confidence, had time to reconsider.

But, of course, if it was up to Paulette, she'd never get that opportunity—unless she could wrest the job from Rob without her sibling's knowledge and prove to the family once and for all she could do it.

Back in the kitchen, she opened a can of mixed fruit and sat down to eat while perusing her mother's stack of *Good Housekeeping*. But an hour later she realized she'd glanced solely at the photos, none of the text. Her mind was too preoccupied with plotting how she could convince her parents she was here to stay this time—and troubling over Rob McGuire's uncharacteristic behavior.

While he'd always fully focused on whatever goal

was set before him, he used to be easygoing. Sure, he'd been a serious thinker back then, but now he was *serious.* The Rob of old never would have cut off a friendly overture with a remark like that.

A chirping sound echoed through the kitchen. She tracked it to a cell phone—tucked under a philodendron's foliage—where it must have slid from Paulette's purse. She snatched it up and punched what she hoped was the right button.

"Hello?"

There was a hesitation on the other end. "Paulette?"

She recognized the voice and caught her breath. "This is Olivia."

Another pause. "This is Rob McGuire. Would you please put her on?"

"She left without her phone. Could I get a message to her?"

He hesitated again and she envisioned him raking a hand through his sun-streaked hair, a familiar gesture she remembered well. "After what happened at Timberline, I decided to check out the rest of the property. And there's a problem."

"Meaning?"

"Meaning someone tagged Bristlecone."

"They did what?"

"Spray-painted graffiti on interior walls," he clarified in a tight voice. "And *your* name figures prominently in the artwork."

* * *

"I should have asked her to have Paulette call me. That's it." Grumbling aloud, Rob dug around in the property's Jeep Wrangler, trying to find his pen.

He wasn't required to bring the oldest Diaz daughter up to speed on Singing Rock business, but she'd asked him to keep her in the loop while her parents were gone. Wanting to stay on the good side of a woman he suspected could influence the outcome of this new venture, he'd indulged her. He didn't think she questioned his authority, but sought to protect her parents' rare time off. She needn't have worried. This sort of thing didn't warrant, in his estimation, a call to Paul and Rosa.

But now Olivia was on her way, insisting she needed to take a look at the damage he'd unthinkingly brought to her attention. He hadn't missed the earlier dismay that crossed her pretty, animated features when he told her he was the new manager. Almost as if she didn't think him sufficiently competent to handle it. Which was a real turnaround from what he could remember of her now that he'd had time to think about it.

Back in college she always seemed to show up when he least expected it. An idealistic, high-spirited sprite, trying hard to get his attention. Hanging on his every word. Thinking he could do no wrong.

His stomach twisted at the sound of an approaching vehicle. Probably hers. He sucked in a weary breath. *Do no wrong.* She'd been way off base on that one. And yet, after all this time, he wasn't keen on setting her straight.

Letting her down.

It had taken her all of five minutes to pull on a pair of jeans and head out to check on the situation herself. Mr. McGuire might not appreciate her interference or the return of the good old days, but she'd promised herself to look out for things in her parents' absence. So like it or not, he'd better get used to it. Managing Singing Rock was her heritage, not his.

Spotting the cabin through the pines, one of twenty scattered across Singing Rock's thickly treed acreage that backed up to forest service property, she tightened her grip on the steering wheel as she eased the nose of her car off the rutted road. She hadn't thought about Rob more than a time or two—okay, or two thousand—in the past seven years. So what was with the anticipatory butterflies bouncing around in her stomach?

Up a slight rise hunkered the well-remembered cabin with its log and native stone facade, shingled roof and rustic wooden porch. Natural rock chimneys graced opposite ends of the structure and a half-barrel of fuchsia petunias squatted near the steps. An open-topped, black Jeep Wrangler sat off to one side. Just like the property's other SUV, its door was emblazoned with "Singing Rock Cabin Resort—Canyon Springs, Arizona."

As if on cue, Rob emerged from its interior, shading his eyes from the sun's glare piercing through the canopy of pine branches. With a frown, he peeled out of his windbreaker and tossed it to the seat. Then slipping a pair of sunglasses on, he strode toward her as she exited her vehicle.

She couldn't see his eyes, hidden as they were behind his sunglasses, but she felt them on her. What did he see when he looked at her? The skinny, giggling freshman she'd been—or the woman she hoped she'd become?

She took a deep breath to quiet her thumping heart. *Get a grip, Olivia. You're not a starry-eyed eighteen-year-old anymore.* She flashed him a bright smile as he came to a halt before her, determined that Mr. Grumpy wasn't going to ruin *her* day. "Now where's this graffiti you called about?"

Rob's brows rose over the top of his shades and for a moment she thought he was going to tell her there was no need to trouble herself, he'd handle it. But then he tilted his head and swept his arm toward the cabin in an almost deferential invitation.

When she hesitated, he set off on the trail to the log structure, anyway, leaving her to trot along behind. It was apparent he didn't plan to allow their so-called reunion to be anything more than superficial. Which was total silliness. His romantic blunder happened over seven years ago. *Get over it, Rob.*

Without warning, a squirrel shot out of the timber and across their path, a youthful black Labrador retriever in hot pursuit.

"Elmo." Rob's sharp tone and a palm slapped against his denim-clad thigh caught the pup's attention. The dog skittered to an uncertain halt, his head swiveling from his escaping playmate to Rob and back again. Then he ducked his head and approached, body quivering and tail wagging, to throw himself in humble adoration at Rob's feet.

Olivia could relate.

She crouched to pat the puppy. It seemed to be all tongue at the moment, and she fended off a flurry of wet kisses. "What a doll. He's yours?"

"My assistant manager's. I'll have to remind him about the property's leash rules."

He had an assistant manager? How'd he rate that?

"A cutie for sure. How old is he?"

Rob's brow crinkled. "Early to mid-thirties probably. And I thought he was kind of an ugly dude myself."

She laughed and fended off another onslaught of exuberant puppy passion, her heart lightening. So the man did still have a sense of humor buried under that hands-off demeanor. "Very funny."

"Oh, you meant the *pooch?*" Rob didn't so much as crack a smile. But she sensed it there. Lurking. She'd get one out of him yet. "He's five or six months old."

The squirming pup rolled onto its back for a belly rub, his ID tags jingling. She obliged, glancing up at Rob, but his expression remained unreadable behind the dark-tinted glasses. After a long moment and without a word, he turned and again walked toward the cabin. Clambering to her feet, Olivia dusted herself off, gave Elmo a final pat, then trailed His Royal Highness through the trees, dried pine needles and pinecones crunching under the soles of her flip-flops.

The Rob of her dreams this was not.

What's happened to him, Lord?

The dog romped back and forth between them, coming close to tripping her a time or two.

"Elmo." Rob snapped his fingers and pointed at the ground. "Sit."

The pup plopped down on its bottom, tail wagging and feet kneading the ground. He took a tentative step and Rob repeated the command. The Lab reseated himself, whimpering as they moved on. She gave the little guy a sympathetic glance. But when it was clear there would be no more pats and tummy rubs, his ears perked up and he sprang to his feet. Raced back through the forest to new adventures.

"He's adorable."

"I guess so. But his boundless enthusiasm can be a pain."

Her heart jolted, recalling the tone of Paulette's

scathing indictment. *You can't come bounding in here with your typical puppy-dog enthusiasm, straining a working relationship with Mom and Dad's new manager.*

She glanced at Rob. Was that how he viewed her, too?

But it appeared he wasn't paying any attention to her whatsoever as they ascended the railroad tie steps to the cabin. Joining him on the porch, she turned to gaze out at the breathtaking view, glimpsing a distant low mountain between a gap in the thick stand of pines.

"I've always loved this cabin." Opening her arms wide as if to embrace the property, she inhaled the scent of sun-warmed pine. Then immediately dropped her arms to her sides, self-conscious of appearing too enthusiastic.

Rob's brow lowered. "I suppose you grew up here. On the Singing Rock property as a whole, I mean."

You can knock off with the frowning, thank you.

"You suppose right."

Forehead puckered, he pocketed his sunglasses and cocked his head. "Has it changed much through the years?"

Pinned by his gaze, she floundered for an analysis worthy of his now-interested attention.

"Changed? Yes and no."

Kinda like you, Robby.

Chapter Three

He folded his arms, skepticism in his tone. "Yes *and* no?"

"Mom and Dad expanded it through the years." She loved extolling all they'd done to make Singing Rock what it was today. "They built on what Grandma and Grandpa—Mom's parents—started out with. Added cabins. The lodge. But basically, it's the same in essence as it always has been. Guests have come to expect that."

"You think so?"

Why was he challenging her? Acting like he didn't know what she was talking about?

"Sure. Singing Rock's been around for sixty-some years. There are even people who've been coming here every summer for five decades of those."

"The Millards, right? Your folks mentioned they celebrated their fiftieth wedding anniversary at the lodge last year."

"See what I mean? Singing Rock's a family tradition." She caught his furrowed frown and laughed. "You doubt that?"

"What's Singing Rock doing to attract the Millards' grandkids? Great-grandkids?"

Pride swelled. "Exactly what we've always done. Opening our hearts—and our cabins—to share genuine high country hospitality."

Rob braced an arm on a porch support post. "Don't get me wrong. I understand and appreciate that sentiment. But unfortunately, that doesn't cut it in today's market. A lot of people are looking to have their days scheduled with diverse activities. Add to that a growing desire for more amenities. Conveniences. Luxuries even."

"Like cable TV and free internet access? A gourmet coffee shop on site?" She shook her head. It looked like she had a lot to do yet to educate Rob. "Mom and Dad pride themselves on limiting the influence of that kind of thing. They believe you should be your own entertainment."

"But those kinds of people aren't keeping the cabins full, now are they?"

Why was he being so obstinate?

"Maybe not in this economic slump. But that's the whole reason people come to Singing Rock." She motioned toward the captivating view from the porch. "They'd rather commune with God and nature than sit in front of an electronic screen of some variety.

They want to get themselves and their kids away from all-consuming technology and flee the stuff that causes them stress on a daily basis. The place that delivers on that promise is Singing Rock."

Rob tilted his head. "A good cup of coffee causes stress?"

"A good cup of coffee doesn't have to cost five or six bucks a pop. That *does* cause stress." She studied him a long moment, an uneasiness floating around the edges of her mind. She folded her arms. "You're not thinking of trying to talk my folks into that kind of junk are you? I can tell you right now it won't fly."

"Coffee shop? No way. But it's your parents who asked me to evaluate how Singing Rock can be brought into the twenty-first century. As I'm sure you're already aware, business sagged notably the past few years."

"That's due to a general dip in the economy." Or had Mom and Dad suffered a financial blow? Was that what Paulette meant when she referred to the future of Singing Rock being on the line? "Everyone's taking a hit, right?"

"The Evergreen property up the road is holding its own, staying filled. Each unit has internet, widescreen TV. They offer a pool, tennis court, exercise room, buffet breakfast—"

With a laugh she held up a restraining hand. "Wait, wait, wait. Kyle Marsh's place? Are you kidding me? That condo kingdom that comes complete with cute garages so the sports cars won't get coated with pine pollen or spotted with sticky ponderosa sap? You can't compare our place to his."

"Why not? He's the competition."

She placed her hands on her hips, but kept her smile steady. "No, he's not. Kyle wouldn't know a trout from a goldfish. A canoe from a surfboard. And his upscale clientele couldn't care less about that type of thing, either. That's not the crowd Singing Rock caters to."

"Maybe not currently, but—"

"There are already enough places to accommodate that other demographic. The heart of the high country is in the outdoors—fishing, hiking, stargazing. Sing-a-alongs and marshmallow roasts around a campfire."

She shook her head, struggling not to laugh again. "Look, Rob, I assure you, Kyle's place isn't what Mom and Dad were alluding to when they asked you for recommendations. They'll expect estimates on a redo of the sand volleyball lot, digging new fire pits, re-rocking the parking areas or replacing worn-out porch furniture. Do you have any idea what internal turmoil they went through before deciding it would be acceptable to put microwaves in the cabins? To build a website?"

He frowned. Again.

"So," she said, before he could sing more praises of neighboring Evergreen. Her folks would faint dead away. "Should we take a look at this piece of artwork you called about?"

His mouth set in a grim line, Rob pushed open the glass-paned wooden door and motioned her inside. The faint, comforting scent of wood smoke and cinnamon greeted them as they stepped onto the hardwood floors of the shadowed interior. It took a moment for her daylight-accustomed eyes to adjust to the dimmer surroundings. But there was no mistaking the colorful scrawl across the cream-colored wall inside the entryway.

"NO MORE," it proclaimed in three-foot-high letters.

"No more what?" While concerned about the defacement of the charming space and the effort it would take to remedy the perpetrator's handiwork, a rush of relief flooded her. "I thought you said *my* name figured into this."

Rob came from behind and gripped her shoulders, turning her to the left. "That's your name, isn't it?"

DIAZ. With a bright crimson slash through it.

"That may be my last name," she protested with a shot of apprehension as Rob released her. "But this doesn't have anything to do with me. Did you call the deputy again?"

Rob stepped back, gazing at the wall with a critical eye. "Not yet."

"But you're going to, right?"

He rubbed a hand along the back of his neck, a

weary gesture. "It will delay getting the place re-painted. I have guests for this unit arriving Friday afternoon."

Should she override his decision and make the call to law enforcement herself? Was it wise to challenge Rob's authority so early in their renewed acquaintance? What if he told Paulette?

"Shouldn't we get this on record? It isn't a random act if someone knows my parents' name. It's like a personal threat."

He met her gaze, continuing to massage his neck. "More like a major irritant. But as I told the deputy this morning, I suspect what's been going on is a calling card left by the environmentally-minded kids I had a run-in with the first week I got here. They were well-intentioned high schoolers, up from Phoenix for the summer, would be my guess. Took exception to a tree-thinning project your folks have going along the highway side of the property to lower the risk of a major fire."

"Wouldn't they be back in school by now?"

"Not if they go to a private one. You know, an independent. Lots of those around these days that don't start until after Labor Day. But if that's the case, we should be rid of them after this weekend."

"Can't you have them arrested?"

"I didn't recognize them as kids staying here, and they've kept themselves scarce since I warned them off." He squared his shoulders. "But I can't afford to lose out on the weekend's revenue by delaying repairs. In studying the records, I noticed that except for the Fourth of July, this will be the first time this year that we'll come close to having a full house. I have a couple of days to get Timberline and Bristlecone back in guest-ready condition, and standing here debating the issue is cutting into that time."

"Still—"

"I guarantee you that the deputy has more important things to see to with the holiday approaching. Wouldn't be too happy to hear from either of us for something this minor."

She couldn't argue with him on that point. But what would Mom and Dad do if they were here? She pulled her cell phone from where she'd clipped it to the waistband of her jeans and switched it to camera mode. "I'd at least like to get photos. In case we need evidence later."

"Suit yourself."

She fully intended to. And it was becoming quite clear she'd better keep an eye on Rob—in her parents' best interests, of course.

He'd ticked her off.

He could tell by the way her chin jutted and those beautiful eyes flashed that she thought he should drag the deputy back out here. But that was a waste of everyone's time. Time he certainly didn't have to spare.

She didn't seem to be in any hurry with the photos, clicking away from different angles to ensure good snapshots of the vandalized walls. But it gave him a few minutes to step out of her way, to strategize. He didn't know how much influence she had on her parents' decision-making, but it probably wasn't a smart move to alienate her. He'd been caught off guard when she'd reminded him of their college connection. Hadn't been thinking clearly when he'd told her he had no intention of joining her for a walk down memory lane.

He still couldn't risk getting too friendly. But there had to be a satisfactory middle ground.

He shot her a covert glance. Dainty little thing, but the coltish figure he remembered from the church volleyball team had filled out and the carelessly cropped hair now tumbled down her back. The once-sharp planes of her face had softened. No wonder he hadn't recognized her when she'd stepped out on the porch earlier that morning.

She'd grown up, that was for sure.

Which was exactly why he had to walk a fine line here. Couldn't encourage her to hang around. But neither could he again deliver an ill-thought-out comment like the one he'd made earlier in hopes of keeping her at bay. A move he'd have to make up for.

"Olivia…"

"Hang on. I'm almost done."

"Take your time."

She lowered her phone and spun toward him as if surprised. Had she been dawdling just to irritate him?

He met her questioning gaze. "You're right. It's a good idea to take photos. And if you think your parents would call the county about this, I can do that."

Confusion flitted through her eyes. "No, that's all right. Like you said, there's nothing for the deputy to see that he can't analyze in a few good photos."

"If you're sure." He ducked his head and again rubbed a hand along his neck, hoping she didn't detect his relief. Now he could get to that painting without delay. He glanced back at her. "And I'm sorry about earlier this morning."

She tilted her head in question.

"You know, when you mentioned catching up on our college days? I really didn't mean to sound so—" He paused, fishing for an appropriate word.

"Rude?" she asked brightly.

His startled gaze bored into hers. "It *was* rude, wasn't it?"

She scrunched her face. "Mmm. On a scale of one to ten, I'd give it a twelve since it was in front of my big sister."

"Hey, I'm really sorry. I won't make excuses, but please don't take it personally. It's just that—"

"Look, Rob." Her eyes filled with a puzzling sympathy as she stepped forward to lay a reassuring hand on his arm. "You don't need to worry that I'll say anything to anyone about…well, you know."

The muscles in his throat constricted. How did she—?

"It's no one else's business that Gretchen dumped you in front of God and everybody. It was a long time ago." She cut him a mischievous look. "And besides, we're all entitled to look like an idiot once in a while, right?"

Time stood still as he stared at her, trying to assimilate her words. Then he threw back his head and laughed. Gretchen. She thought his ill-at-ease behavior was about Gretchen. *Thank You, God.* Of course she wouldn't know about anything that had transpired since their NAU days.

Wonderment lighting her face, she laughed, too, apparently relieved to see him taking her blunt comment so well.

After several more moments of unconstrained laughter, he wiped at an eye, chuckled and shook his head, getting himself under control. "Oh, man. An idiot, huh? Thank you, Olivia, for sharing that tender sentiment with me. It's always good to know how old acquaintances feel about you."

She gazed up at him, face aglow with the almost-worshipful expression he remembered from college.

It sunk his momentary relief like a rock.

Olivia's heart did a loop-de-loop as she got an unexpected glimpse of the Rob of old—the flash of even white teeth and gray eyes dancing in merriment. It was the first unrestrained response she'd gotten out of him. And boy, was it worth the wait.

"I've had more than my share of public humiliations," she assured, smiling up at him and marveling at the transformation. Maybe Paulette was right. His bad experience in Vegas had driven him inside himself. Put him on his guard.

Now she'd have to figure out a way to keep him from retreating again. She'd have to be fast. The light in his eyes had already dimmed.

"So where's the paint, huh?" She looped her arm through his, feeling him flinch as her bare arm made contact with his rock-solid one.

"You want to paint?"

"Sure. What else do I have to do today?"

"Maybe see your family? Relax? That's what vacations are for, right?"

She shrugged, not wanting to explain why she'd come back to Canyon Springs. He might not take it kindly that her plans included worming her way back into Singing Rock management. "There's plenty of time to fulfill familial obligations."

"Well, then—" He slipped out of her light grasp and stepped away, almost as if relieved to put some distance between them. "I have primer and paint back at the lodge. Rollers, brushes and drop cloths."

Gazing happily at him, she winked. "So let's get to it, Mr. McGuire."

And knock off with the frowning.

* * *

"How's it going up there in the Northland, Rob?" His mom's words echoed through the cell phone as slivers of Wednesday morning's dawn penetrated the thick stand of pines. Cloudless sky at the moment, but end-of-monsoon-season rains filled the forecast. "Is Canyon Springs everything Meg painted it to be?"

Settling himself on the lodge's porch steps, he took a sip from his coffee, savoring the warmth on this chilly morning. Hard to believe overnight lows could be in the fifties this time of year. His little sister had made a big deal about the cool, more-than-a-mile-high-elevation summers in Canyon Springs. Sure beat baking under a desert sun.

"Haven't really gotten out that much in the community, Mom. An errand here and there. But it's beautiful country. And everyone seems friendly enough."

Not too nosy.

He took another sip of coffee as his gaze took in the forest clearing—Paul and Rosa's cabin, still dark at this early hour—and their youngest daughter's silver coupe parked outside. While his sister sang the praises of small-town America, assuring him Canyon Springs was the cure for whatever ailed you, she'd failed to mention her husband's attractive, vivacious cousin in that portrait of the community she'd wooed him with.

He'd done his best to keep as far from Olivia as he could while priming the damaged cabin walls yesterday morning. But over and over she'd invaded his personal space, standing too close, brushing against his arm. Talking, smiling, laughing the whole time—and dragging him in on it—totally oblivious of the fact he'd rather be left alone.

"Do you see Meg often?" His mother's voice drew him back to the present, away from memories of the sunny animation that characterized Olivia Diaz.

"Like I've said before, she's teaching and it's hard for me to get away from here. But she and Davy brought me dinner Monday night when Joe was out working his shift, and we enjoyed catching up. She's sure loving that stepson of hers. And she glows when she talks about her job and Joe."

"Good. But I hope her feelings about the town haven't given you unrealistic expectations. She tends to see it through rose-colored glasses."

"Don't worry, Mom. You know me, my feet are planted firmly on the ground."

She didn't immediately reply and the silence stretched.

"What?" he pressed, not certain he wanted to hear what she had on her mind.

"Little towns talk."

He took a deep breath and set the mug on the porch. "I know."

"I don't want to see you hurt, honey."

"I don't want that, either. But Vegas, Phoenix—any big city—they're out of the question now."

"You're still having trouble dealing with what happened."

No point in denying it.

"Try having a gun put to your head and see how you'd be doing." He forced a chuckle, hoping to allay his mother's concern. But he squeezed his eyes shut as the muscles in his stomach tightened and he broke out in a light sweat. Just as he did each time he relived the cold steel pressed against his temple— remembered what he'd come so close to losing. "But I like the job. I like what I've seen of the town. My employers are putting their faith in me and I intend to deliver."

He heard a disturbance in the background at the other end of the line. A familiar, plaintive, high-pitched voice. Then his mother's reassuring murmurs. Her laugh.

"There's someone here who wants to talk to you, Rob."

"Put her on." His spirits rose in anticipation.

More commotion. The sound of the phone being dropped. Recovered. Then a heavy breathiness coming through the receiver, pulsing warmly across the miles.

"Is that you, Angie?" he teased, his heart warming. He lived for these phone calls. "What are you doing up so early, pumpkin?"

A giggle tickled his ears.

"Daddy!"

Chapter Four

No doubt about it, Rob was trying to avoid her.

When they'd finished painting at Bristlecone yesterday, he turned down her invitation for a jaunt to Camilla's Café for lunch. Looking uncomfortable, he'd hustled off, claiming he had an important phone call to make. She hadn't seen him the rest of the day. In fact, not until a short while ago when he settled himself on the steps of the lodge's front porch.

Peeking from behind a lacy curtain at her folks' house, she'd watched as he pulled out his cell phone and dived into a conversation as he savored his morning coffee. The chat appeared to start out light, then got serious. But by the time it wrapped up, he seemed in a good mood. Smiling. Laughing. Even with the window open, she couldn't hear specific words from across the clearing. He kept his voice low. But she could hear his teasing tones. The laugh.

A business call? Not likely. Unless girlfriend business.

Which would explain a lot of things. Like why, although he apologized about his earlier brusque behavior, he still hadn't encouraged anything but conversational superficialities. Certainly no "remember when" stuff. He'd remained pretty much Mr. Sobersides. Still seemed on edge even when they'd gotten that Gretchen issue out of the way. He'd laughed about that. Seemed to loosen up. Then shut down again.

Maybe his girlfriend was the jealous type, whose ire he didn't want to raise by mentioning an old college acquaintance—a female one at that. A clingy, suspicious woman didn't deserve a man like Rob. Two-timing wasn't in his vocabulary. Squeaky-clean. Principled. High standards both for himself and others. If you couldn't trust a guy like that, who could you trust? If his lady friend had reservations about the very foundation that made up Rob McGuire, she didn't stand a chance of hanging on to him for long.

Which meant he might soon be in the market for a new one?

When he shut off his cell and reentered the lodge, Olivia dashed off to don a sweatshirt, then rushed across the clearing. Her timing coincided with him coming out again and heading to the Jeep. He certainly looked more than fine this morning in that blue chambray shirt, jeans and work boots.

She stopped not far from him, slipping her hands into her back pockets. "Hey, Rob."

"You're an early bird." His low voice rumbled, as if not yet quite awake.

"Ready for Timberline, how about you?"

From the uncertainty flickering through his eyes, he'd obviously hoped he could slip off without being seen. "Plenty to do out there. But you know what would help me most?"

She shook her head. Whatever it was, she'd deliver.

"I could use a few things from town, if you wouldn't mind running an errand for me." He pulled out his wallet, peeled off half a dozen twenties and handed them to her along with a slip of paper containing his compact script.

Yep. He was trying to avoid her.

She flashed him a perky smile, not letting on that she knew this was busywork to get her out of his hair—an effort to appease his green-eyed girlfriend. The list did seem legitimate. Not too extensive. Items for cleaning and repair work.

"I think you can get everything at the discount house. Or Dix's Woodland Warehouse may have some of it, too. I imagine both will be open even this early in the morning."

She stuffed the bills into the front pocket of her

jeans, then studied the list more closely. "No substitutes for the brands you have here?"

"Not if you can help it."

"I'll call if I can't find your first choice. Let you decide from what's available. What's your cell number?" She hadn't thought to get it off Paulette's phone.

Without hesitation, he handed her a Singing Rock business card. Main phone number, address, website. His name and personal cell number.

"Thanks." She tucked it in her back pocket. If he already had cards printed up, proclaiming him to be the property's manager, it appeared he had a long-term stint in mind. Which could be problematic.

"From the list you gave Paulette earlier, it looked as if the damage was more extensive at Timberline than Bristlecone."

"Considerably. Bristlecone was a paint job. But Timberline has a busted lock. Broken window. Totally trashed, like Pinyon. A least these incidents should be the last of it."

"You mean if it's those kids who'll head home after the holiday weekend?"

"Right. Then maybe we'll have peace and quiet around here." Rob turned toward the Jeep.

"I'll bring everything straight out to Timberline."

"You don't have to do that. Set everything inside the side door of the office. Give me a call and I'll pick it up. I don't want you spending your whole vacation on Singing Rock repairs."

Or following him around?

Rob seemed under the impression she'd be here for Labor Day weekend, then on her way. Or was that wishful thinking on his part?

"It's no trouble. Besides, I'd like to look at the damage."

"May not be much to see by the time you return." At least he politely refrained from pointing out that she'd turned down the opportunity to look it over when the deputy suggested it. "I made some headway on it yesterday afternoon. If I get the mess cleaned up, I can move on to the repairs faster."

Not knowing he'd intended to jump ahead on the clean up without her yesterday, she'd run errands, stocked up on groceries and returned Paulette's phone to her. Why hadn't she thought to inspect Timberline first? What if her folks called? How could she report knowledgably on the situation, like a manager would do, if she couldn't provide an eyewitness evaluation?

She glanced at the list again. "This shouldn't take too long. Maybe you'll still need help by the time I get back."

He frowned—surprise, surprise—then nodded. "Suit yourself."

Suit yourself. That seemed to be his standard, noncommittal response to her suggestions. Undoubtedly he'd get that cabin cleaned up and repaired in record time, ensuring little remained for her to assist with. But she was a power shopper, not given to lingering in the aisles like many ladies loved to do. She preferred to have a list in hand and get in and get out.

So they'd see who beat whom….

Rob glanced at his watch again, then toward the center of the cabin's main room piled high with debris he'd gathered from the wreckage. Why did things always take longer than you thought they would? Olivia would be back before he knew it.

As at Pinyon last week, malicious visitors had done their best to render the space uninhabitable. Fortunately, except for the lock and window, damage was relatively superficial, but time-consuming to clean up.

When he'd worked for a Flagstaff property management business in college, he'd seen far worse. Whoever had done this was an amateur by comparison. At least here cement hadn't been poured down the toilet to harden.

But it was a mess nevertheless. Feathers from sliced-up pillows floated around like snowy confetti and the contents of salt, pepper, coffee and sugar containers covered the floor in a gritty coating. If he'd have been smart, he'd have done the in-town errands himself and assigned Olivia to tackle the cleaning. Or rousted out his part-time assistant manager to wield the mop and vacuum, even if it was his day off.

On his drive out to Timberline, he'd rechecked the other vacant cabins. Found another "tagged" overnight. A back door window pane had been broken where they could reach in and unlock the door. Like here, coffee packet contents had been strewn about along with sugar and salt. Not trashed as badly as this one, but so much for hopes that they'd seen the last of the hooligans.

He'd told Olivia he suspected kids were the culprits. But he couldn't be certain of that. He didn't like to think it might be the beginning of something more serious. These cabins farthest from the Singing Rock lodge hadn't been occupied for the past month or more. Had they become handy hideouts for adults with more criminal intent?

The muscles in his upper arms tightened at the thought of walking blindly into another situation like the one of a month-and-a-half ago. He hurled a battered foam pillow to the growing pile of debris, the abrupt, fierce motion momentarily easing the tension in his shoulders.

"You're letting yourself get spooked, bud," he muttered aloud. Hadn't Paul and Rosa shown him around the property when he'd come for the interview a few weeks ago? He'd ventured out this way on his own since then, too. None of those times had there been evidence of recent occupation. No tell-tale signs or scents that might accompany alcohol or drug use. Drug manufacturing.

No, it had to be those kids. Well-intentioned teens who feared that tree thinning and the related loss of the thick undergrowth between the pines would reduce ground cover for small animals. Admittedly, it would for a time. But it also served as a safeguard against a massive conflagration. He'd been witness to the devastation caused by lightning or abandoned campfires in mountain country. Hundreds, thousands or even hundreds of thousands of acres of pristine ponderosa pine forest reduced to charred rubble. Nothing remaining to harbor any animal, feathered or furry, for a good hundred years or more.

He could handle the kids. But the thought of adult trespassers gnawed at his mind. Only weeks ago, when he'd walked out of the interview with a job offer, Canyon Springs seemed an answered prayer. Ideal for raising his precious two-year-old daughter, Angela.

Sweet Angie.

A smile tugged at the corner of his mouth as he recalled her wispy brown hair. Soft, flawless skin. Big gray eyes focused trustingly on him, her tiny hand cradled in his.

His hands fisted. He'd protect her with his dying breath.

Had it just been a few weeks ago as he'd lain in bed awaiting the blare of the alarm clock, that he'd meditated on the comforting realization that for the first time in a long time he'd listened for and heard God's voice? Had obediently walked through the door he believed God opened. But now his decision seemed tainted. Criminal activity shattered the illusion of safety.

He glanced at the open door as his ears picked up the crunch of gravel from an approaching vehicle. The sound of an engine shutting off. The slam of a door.

Olivia. How could she be back so soon? It wasn't even nine o'clock. He took a deep breath.

"Rob! Rob!"

A prickling sensation raced up his spine at the desperation in her voice. He launched himself out the front door.

"Hurry, Rob!"

Olivia jumped up from where she knelt beside a shivering and bloodied Elmo. She took a quick step toward the cabin, then halted. Swung back toward the whimpering animal whose soulful brown eyes focused on her. She dropped again to her knees beside the crouching pup, its tail wagging a half-hearted greeting. And then Rob was there beside her.

"What happened? Did you hit him?"

What kind of assumption was that? "No, but it looks like someone did."

With gentle fingers, Rob inspected the pup, cupping its head and lifting it slightly as he bent to get a better look at the damage. "He's got quite a cut here. Look at the dried blood. And it's still oozing."

"Is he going to be okay?" She gave Elmo's flank a reassuring pat.

With a yelp, the pup's head jerked toward her, eyes filled with pain. She yanked her hand back, but the good-natured dog didn't snap at her.

"Looks like that cut isn't his sole problem. We need to get him to a vet." He glanced at her as his bloodied hands stroked the little lab. "I hate to move him, but he's lost considerable blood. Could you run back in there and grab a sheet? There's an old one in the pile on the middle of the floor."

She nodded and staggered to her feet. Inside she found the wadded-up fabric and pulled it free. Raced back to Rob's side.

"Spread it out next to him. Then fold it in half. I'll see if I can lift him onto it without hurting him too much."

She did as she was told. Still on his knees, Rob carefully gathered the whimpering pup into his arms and lowered him onto the cotton cloth.

"You're getting blood all over you."

Rob swiped at the front of his now-stained T-shirt, then brushed his hair back with a forearm, leaving a crimson streak across his forehead.

"Let's get this wrapped around him. Then I'll carry him to the Jeep. I'll drive. You hold him."

She nodded, watching in apprehension as he swaddled Elmo in the sheet and lifted him into his arms. The pup didn't struggle, but she wasn't sure if that was a good sign or bad.

At the open-topped Jeep Wrangler, Rob nodded toward the passenger side of the vehicle. "Hop on in and buckle up."

She obeyed, then he gently lowered the pup onto her lap. Its pitiful little face turned to keep a watchful eye on Rob.

"Got him? He's an armful."

"He's really shaking, isn't he?"

"Probably in shock." Rob took her hand and laid it against the pup's sheet-swathed shoulder. "If you can press firmly right about here, maybe that will slow the blood flow."

Then he gently pushed her knee out of harm's way and slammed the door. Loped to the other side and climbed into the driver's seat. His countenance creased as he glanced at her. "You okay?"

"Yeah."

He nodded in apparent approval as he started the engine, then backed the Jeep enough to swing it around and head for the rock-and-dirt road that wound through the Singing Rock property. Acutely aware of gravel crunching under the tires and the sun dappling through the pines overhead, she adjusted her hold on Elmo as his warm body continued to shiver in her arms. "I wonder what happened to him?"

"No tellin'." Rob eased the vehicle around a sharp corner. "Maybe something fell on him. He's rather accident-prone."

"Is he?" She glanced down at Elmo and gave him a gentle squeeze, praying he'd be okay. "Poor little guy."

The pup lifted his nose and swiped a tongue across her chin. She glanced up in time to see a smile tug at Rob's lips. Where was her camera when she needed it? Record that one for posterity.

He nodded toward the pup. "Looks as if he thinks he's found a friend."

"For life," she said, bracing her feet as they jolted along the rutted, winding road. Passing by another of the property's cabins, its guests relaxing on the porch, she marveled at the day's turn of events. When she'd awakened that morning, never in her wildest dreams would she have imagined she'd be on a rescue mission with an injured dog that wasn't hers. Or with Rob McGuire, for that matter.

He wasn't hers, either.

Yet.

She directed her smile at Elmo. "Hang in there, Rob's going to save you."

Halfway across a creek that snaked through Singing Rock's acreage, the Jeep jerked to a halt on the weathered bridge. Rob stuck his arm out the window, motioning to a muscular, Western-hatted man picking his way along the edge of the water, a fishing pole and tackle box in hand.

"Brett!"

The man, dressed in jeans and a collarless blue knit shirt, waved back with a broad smile. But when Rob crept the Jeep to the other side, it must have registered that the tone and gestures weren't of a happy nature. The man swiftly hopped across the rocks, then scrambled up the embankment, apprehension evident in his features.

"Your mutt got into something again," Rob explained as the man came up to his door. "We're taking him to a vet. You comin'?"

The man's questioning gaze swept to Elmo. Then to her.

Say no. Please, please, please?

She wanted to ride to town with Rob.

Alone.

Chapter Five

"Oh, for cryin'—" Scowling, the cowboy-hatted man moved to Olivia's side of the vehicle to take a closer look at the bundle in her arms. "What is it this time?"

Cradling the pooch, she addressed the man she assumed was Singing Rock's assistant manager. "Not sure. He's got a bad cut. Maybe internal injuries. Or broken bones."

Rob drummed his fingers on the steering wheel. "So, you comin'?"

"Yeah, yeah." The man threw his fishing gear in the back and pulled himself into the rear seat. "I need insurance on that pooch."

"What you need is to keep him on a leash or penned up. Those are the rules."

"Tell that to Elmo. He makes Houdini look like an amateur. Dug out again in the night."

The Jeep jerked as Rob put it in gear, then continued down the narrow, tree-lined road. The other man maneuvered around in the back, getting himself situated before turning his attention to Olivia. He cast her a lopsided, engaging grin. "Rob didn't tell me he had a canine paramedic on staff."

"Olivia, meet Brett Marden, Singing Rock second in command." Rob eased the vehicle to the edge of the highway, leaning forward to look for approaching traffic. "Brett, meet Olivia Diaz. Paul and Rosa's daughter."

"You don't say?" The sandy-haired man's eyebrows rose and he whipped off his Western straw in a respectful gesture. His eyes appraised her in an openly appreciative but inoffensive manner. "Good to meet you, Olivia. Mighty good."

Rob's brows lowered as he turned onto the highway. Ignoring Brett, he looked over at the pup. "How's he doing?"

"Still shivering."

"Lucky dog." Brett resettled his hat on his head, then gave his pet a gentle pat.

"Lucky?" She glanced from Rob to his assistant. "I got the impression from you guys that he is majorly *un*lucky."

"Depends on how you look at it." Brett squinted against the sunshine pouring through the roofless Jeep. "Porcupine quills are the devil to pull out of a sensitive nose. Skunk odors linger forever. But whatever he's done to himself this time managed to get an exceptionally beautiful woman fawning over him. So I'd say it evens out."

Olivia laughed, recognizing a well-practiced flirt. Plenty of fun, but usually not a whole lot of substance.

Rob's forehead creased. Lips tightened. What was his problem? Did he think she wasn't smart enough to spot Brett's over-the-top flattery?

As their speed picked up, wind whipped through the open Jeep and Olivia wished she'd put her hair in a ponytail and donned sunglasses. Ducking her head, she attempted to turn from the cool morning blast, but without success. Long, whiplike strands of hair slapped mercilessly at her eyes and mouth. She squinted, helpless with her hands occupied by the pup. Then from behind, a hand scooped back her unruly mane, holding it in a secure grip.

"Thanks." She cast Brett a grateful smile and received a dimpled one in return.

He winked. "Anytime."

Rob's ever-present frown deepened as he turned off the highway and onto the road leading into town. What was up with him? Like it would kill him to smile once in a while.

The Vegas incident had apparently done a number on him. But if he couldn't loosen up any more than he had thus far—except for that too-short interlude yesterday morning—he'd never make a go of Singing Rock management.

If there was anything she knew about what it took for her folks to run the enterprise successfully, it was that hospitality and flexibility were the keys. Adapting at a moment's notice to whatever came your way. Exuding warmth, acceptance and generosity even when you'd rather slam the door in someone's face. Finding a way to accommodate even the most difficult personalities without showing so much as a hint of annoyance.

Rob flunked that one this morning.

For whatever reason, Brett annoyed him.

Rob glanced at his watch as Olivia and his assistant manager finally reboarded the Jeep—without Elmo. Eleven o'clock. What had taken them so long? After dropping off the pooch, he'd returned to Singing Rock until Olivia called for a pick-up. But from the looks of it, he should have stuck around to chaperone. The pair seemed too cozy, with Brett's arm draped familiarly around Olivia's shoulder when they'd exited the vet's office. Maybe he should warn her. Clue her in to steer clear of the flirtatious ladies' man. After all, she had been his "little sis in Christ" at NAU. Which obligated him to look out for her best interests—and Brett Marden wasn't one of them.

Why were ladies always such suckers for cowboys? Not sure what the attraction was. Must be the hat. Whatever was up between them, though, it was none of his business. She could make her own decisions. She was a grown woman now. Nobody with two eyes in his head could argue with that. Least of all him.

"How's the pup?" Ignoring his assistant, he directed the question to Olivia as she settled her pretty self beside him. Buckled her seat belt. She must have cleaned up at the vet's, as evidence of Elmo's bloody adventure had vanished from her hands and forearms. He'd taken time back at his apartment to clean up, as well. Changed shirts.

"All sewn up. No broken bones. Appear to be no internal injuries. Severe bruising of his hip. But Dr. Sikeston wants to keep him overnight."

"For observation," Brett confirmed.

"She have any idea what happened to him?"

"Said we could be right about a car hitting him sometime in the night." Olivia glanced back at Brett, as if his input mattered. "I'm guessing he heard you at Timberline, Rob, and was making his way there when I found him."

Brett shook his head. "Who'd hit a poor pup and leave him out there like that? Not one of our guests, I hope."

"Same person or persons who'd tear up a cabin. Spray it with graffiti." Rob threw the Jeep in gear, backed out.

"Maybe in the dark they didn't know they'd hit him." As always, Miss Sunshine tried to give the benefit of the doubt. He swung the Jeep around, hit the gas and headed toward the graveled parking lot's exit.

Brett thumped him playfully on the back. "Dude. Let's grab lunch. My treat. A token of appreciation for rescuing that lame-brained mutt of mine."

"That's sweet of you," Olivia's voice all but cooed as she turned, beaming, toward the man ensconced in the backseat.

Rob fought to keep his lip from curling.

"Where to?" Brett prodded. "Kit's Lodge?"

"Ooh, I love Kit's."

He didn't really want to dine with these two. But there was no point in risking coming across like an ungrateful slug. He turned the Jeep in the direction of the popular local eatery. "Works for me. I've learned that when this tightwad offers to foot the bill, you take him up on it."

"Oh, Rob." Olivia laughed, her dark eyes focusing on him. Her smile warmed his heart even as an invisible band tightened around his chest.

The warmth faded, but tension stayed with him throughout their meal as he listened to the light, constant chatter between his college alumna and the cowboy Paul and Rosa hired to assist them prior to his own arrival. Brett was a decent enough guy who, he'd gotten the impression, had been thrown to the ground and stomped on in a recent relationship. He worked hard. Played equally hard. But man, was he a talker. A born charmer. Lit up like fireworks around a pretty woman. By the way Olivia's face glowed and she never stopped smiling, she was eating it up by the bowlful. Between the two of them, Rob couldn't have gotten a word in edgewise if his life depended on it.

"So," Brett continued after a humorous rundown of how he came to acquire Elmo, "do you have pets, Olivia?"

"Not since I was a kid. Living out of a suitcase isn't conducive to that kind of commitment."

"You travel a lot with your job?"

"Jobs. Plural. Odd jobs. Volunteer work. Short-term mission trips, too."

She glanced curiously at Rob—to see if he was listening? Although feigning focus on his meal, he hadn't missed a word.

"Missions, huh?" Brett sat back as he finished off his cherry pie, eyeing her with an unconcealed interest that made Rob want to pop him. "Where at?"

"Latin America. Mexico. American Indian reservations. Most recently Mississippi, helping out after that freaky tornado outbreak."

"Bad stuff," Brett acknowledged, running a thumb around the rim of his coffee cup. "So you like being on the road? Into the adventure?"

Her eyes sparkled. "Love it."

Rob choked down his last bite of apple pie. Out for the adventure. Exploiting the moment. Always on the go, just like his daughter's mother.

Gaze earnest, Brett pushed away his empty plate and folded his forearms on the table's edge. "So exactly what do you do at these places?"

"Sometimes I help build homes. Not much more than shacks by most standards, but a heaven-sent answer for those living in poverty. I'm not so skilled at construction, but enjoy keeping everyone's kids out of the way—occupied with stories about Jesus or helping organize fun and games."

"Well, Olivia," Brett drawled with a slow wink, "you're welcome to organize fun and games for me anytime."

Rob nudged Brett's foot under the table. He'd had enough of this.

Brett grinned. "So, you two knew each other in college, huh?"

"Right." Olivia produced an exaggerated sigh, her eyes shining into Rob's before turning again to Brett. "But sad to say, when we met again he didn't remember me."

Brett cast him a what-kind-of-idiot-are-you look, then gently bumped Olivia's arm with his elbow. "Believe me, I'd have remembered you, Olivia. You can count on that."

Rob managed not to grit his teeth.

"It's not that I didn't remember her. I didn't recognize her." He tossed his napkin to the table. "I think it's time we head back to Singing Rock. It's clouding up and I don't want to get caught in the open Jeep in a downpour. Don't like leaving the property unsupervised for long stretches at a time, either. Particularly with our uninvited guests making themselves at home."

Olivia leaned forward, glancing from one man to another. "Maybe we can set a trap. A sting. Catch 'em in the act."

Brett leaned in, too. "Yeah. A stakeout."

Great. Olivia creeping around the premises in the dark with Brett. "I don't—"

"Olivia, honey." Their gray-haired waitress reached for his now-empty plate, lowering her voice to address the woman across from him. "There's a young couple over there—the booth by the door—asking about honeymoon cabin recommendations for five or six weeks from now. I suggested Singing Rock. You might want to stop by on your way out. Clinch their interest before some other place nabs their business."

Olivia nodded, already getting to her feet. "Thanks for the tip, Sue."

Rising, Rob caught her arm. "Don't you think I should handle this?"

"Why?" She stared at him in apparent confusion. "I've been promoting Singing Rock since I was in diapers."

"Maybe so, but I am the manager now. You're on vacation. Let me handle it."

She gave him a hesitant smile, as if ready to

acquiesce, then slipped her arm from his grasp. "I don't think so."

And off she went.

With a glare at his grinning assistant, he followed behind her.

"I understand you're looking for a cabin to rent," Olivia was saying when he caught up with her at a table where a painfully young-looking couple was seated—with a baby of about three months old, if he judged correctly. It was in a child carrier propped on the booth seat next to the blonde girl.

Honeymoon cabin? Was that what Sue had said?

"For a weekend in October." The mother blushed as she dabbed the baby's sputtering mouth with a napkin. "Our waitress recommended a place called Singing Rock."

"I may be a tiny bit prejudiced, of course," Olivia said with evident pride, "but my parents own that place and I can guarantee you won't be disappointed."

The male half of the couple, not looking much more than a kid himself, held up a brochure of the property he'd extracted from the pile spread out next to his plate—an outdated brochure Rob knew needed a major overhaul. "I picked this up at the chamber of commerce. Looks great. But I'm not sure—" he glanced uncomfortably at his—girlfriend? fiancée? wife? "—you know, if we can swing it."

"You can swing it," Olivia stated without hesitation. "Our busy season falls off after Labor Day, so rates drop. If you stay two nights, we'll throw in the third free."

What? Not until November did they do anything of the sort. Early to mid-October still brought in Valley visitors to enjoy the aspens changing color, warm days and crisp nights. Hunters, too.

"Does that sound good?" she continued, beaming at the surprised couple. "Sue, your waitress, said you're looking for a honeymoon cabin."

"Yes. A honeymoon." The blonde's cheeks flushed again as she motioned to the infant. "We kind of got the cart before the horse, or so my grandma puts it. We're locals—getting married in October when Aiden can take a few days off from his new job."

"Then this calls for a celebration. I have the perfect cabin in mind. Secluded in the pines. Big stone fireplace. Four-poster bed. Spacious deck. Oozes romance. We'll even kick in a candlelight steak dinner catered to your door from right here at Kit's."

What was she doing?

The young woman turned hopeful eyes on her fiancé. "Sounds wonderful, doesn't it?"

"And like an offer we can't refuse." The blonde let out a happy squeal and the boy-man stretched out a hand to Olivia. "Thanks a lot. I'm Aiden Cantra and this is my fiancée, Sally."

"I'm Olivia Diaz." She shook his hand, nodded

to Sally, then turned to Rob. "And this is Rob McGuire...manager of Singing Rock."

He didn't miss the hesitation in her voice before she tagged his title onto the introduction. He grasped the young man's hand. "Looking forward to having you both as guests."

The pair reiterated their thanks and he handed them a business card. After a few more minutes of small talk, he and Olivia left them to finish their meal. Outside the door, he spotted Brett across the parking lot, already in the Jeep. A few steps off the porch, he caught Olivia by the arm and drew her to a halt. Brett didn't need to be privy to this discussion.

Aglow from her good deed, she gazed at him in happy expectation, and for a fleeting moment he almost held his tongue. How'd she get to be so pretty? No, it wasn't solely the pretty part that caught his eye. There were plenty of nice-looking women around. There was something about her that went deeper than that. Something he couldn't quite put his finger on.

Then again, he'd thought there was more to his daughter's mother, too.

He glanced in the direction of the Jeep as thunder rumbled in the distance. He lowered his voice. "I know you mean well, Olivia. But you can't go around doing what you did in there."

Still smiling, she drew back. "Doing what?"

"Cutting special deals. Giving away freebies like

that catered meal. Do you have any idea how much a good steak dinner costs these days? That's lost income."

She laughed, looping her arm through his, and his hope that she'd understood what he was trying to convey faded. "It's an investment, Rob, not an expense. If we make this young couple's dreams come true, they'll be lifetime guests. Their kids and grandkids, too."

"I don't think those two will have much expendable income for quite some time."

"You don't know that," she chided, her light tone indicating she thought he was joking.

"In case you didn't notice, they'd split a single sandwich and an order of fries. Water, not sodas or coffee."

"All the more reason to give them a break. Besides, don't you think people should be rewarded for doing the right thing?"

"What right thing?"

"You know, the kid." Her eyes glistened with happiness, a dimple surfacing in her cheek. "Getting married. Not leaving a baby to make its way in the cold cruel world without a committed, two-parent family."

His stomach wrenched as his precious Angie's countenance flashed through his mind.

Breathe, McGuire, breathe.

"I— It's the right thing," he said slowly, determined not to let on that the air had nearly been sucked from his lungs, "if Aiden's not a lousy father and Sally an even lousier mother."

"Oh, come on, Rob. How did you get to be such a cynic?" She tugged on his arm, her disbelieving smile evidence she still wasn't taking him seriously. "I have a good feeling about those two. I want to reward them for not running from responsibility. For committing to each other and the baby. For thinking about someone else besides themselves."

Tension mounting in his shoulders, he eased his arm from her grasp. "Don't make a habit of this give-away stuff, okay? Not without my approval."

"*Your* approval?" She made a sound of exasperation. "Look, Rob, this is my folks' place. I know how they like to do business. I'm not going to run around town passing out freebies to everyone I meet. But I have a vested interest in Singing Rock, an even more pressing need for its success than you do."

"How's that?"

"This is my parents' legacy of hard work and personal sacrifice. And my mom's parents before them. So think whatever you want, but recognize I'm not going to let your personal agenda for Singing Rock— whatever it may be—change the mission my folks established for it."

So she didn't plan to cooperate.

"Nevertheless—" He forced more backbone into

his tone. "I'm asking that you not do anything like that again without asking me."

The light in her eyes momentarily dimmed, then flared again. Another growl of distant thunder echoed. "Do you have any idea how many times I've seen my dad do the same thing I did in Kit's? Bring a smile to those who might have no reason to smile? My folks not only tithe with their money, but with their time and their possessions—of which Singing Rock is an integral one."

"I understand tithing. And I respect your parents' choices. But I believe they'd agree with me—and would be biblically well-grounded in doing so—that God doesn't expect you to give away something that isn't yours to give."

"What are you saying?" Her eyes searched his. "Are you telling me Singing Rock is in danger of financial collapse? This is the second time you've alluded to that."

At last. He'd finally gotten her attention.

"Not immediately. But your parents have to invest in the property wisely to garner stronger returns in the future. Singing Rock's cabins are only eighty percent full this summer. On top of that, most places around here—your folks' included—have had to discount their rentals by twenty percent during this recession. Indiscriminate tossing away of potential revenue—*by their daughter*—could snowball into a less than desirable outcome."

Her dark eyes flickered. "They'd have told me if there was any danger of that. And they certainly wouldn't have hired *you* and gone gallivanting off on vacation if that were the case."

"In spite of their hiring me to breathe new life into Singing Rock, I'm actually not certain your folks entirely grasp the seriousness of the situation."

She lifted her chin. "I'm not going to let you scare me."

He silently counted to ten. "I'm not trying to scare you. I'm trying to help you understand the situation. So please, in the future consult me if you get a whim to make special offers. I have only a matter of weeks to come up with a plan that will get this ship, this *Titanic,* turned before it hits an iceberg."

Lightning flared in the still-far-off darkening clouds. Another thunder roll, the scent of rain, accompanied by the disheartening realization that if Olivia refused to cooperate, he didn't stand a chance.

Chapter Six

He might deny it, but she knew deep down that Rob was trying to spook her. Trying to keep her from involving herself in the running of Singing Rock.

Things couldn't be as bad as he'd made it sound. She had nothing to be afraid of—unless he told Paulette what she'd done. That she'd sashayed over to that young couple at Kit's and right under the current manager's nose gave them a special deal. Even if Paulette agreed that's something she'd witnessed Dad do a million times, she would come down on her hard for interfering with Singing Rock business.

But she didn't dare call her parents to get to the truth of Rob's allegations. Couldn't risk reminding them of the responsibilities they were escaping for a few weeks. Paulette would kill her. She'd responded cheerfully to a text message from Mom that morning, not even mentioning she was at Singing Rock.

Now, sitting in the swing of the darkened front

porch late that night, keeping an eye on the lighted window of the apartment above the lodge, she pressed a speed-dial number on her cell phone.

"Hey, Rey."

"Olivia!" The voice of Reyna Kenton—pastor's wife and sister number four of the five Diaz girls—bubbled over with delight. "I wondered when I'd hear from you. Paulette told Lara who told Claire who told me that she'd seen you at Singing Rock yesterday. We weren't expecting you. I guess Mom and Dad didn't know you were coming, either?"

"I'd hoped to surprise them."

"Some surprise, huh? So are you here through the holiday weekend? When do you have to be back at work?"

"I'm between jobs."

"Oh, Olivia." The disappointment resounded in her sister's tone. "This was the organization that's helping out in the aftermath of the tornadoes, right? What happened this time? Not a good fit?"

She took a ragged breath. "Job was fine. The new supervisor, Kendal Paige, wasn't."

"Details, please."

Olivia curled her legs up next to her. "I'd been dating him for over a month when one afternoon in walks a woman with three kids in tow. All four of them bouncing off the walls with excitement because they'd driven straight through from El Paso—to surprise hubby and daddy. Does my luck stink or what?"

"Oh, Liv. You had no idea he was married? None whatsoever? How could you not—"

"Rey, I've gone over every second of those weeks from the moment he first joined the team. Nothing. No hints. No telltale signs. Nothing to make me suspicious. Except—"

"Except what?"

"He didn't want the team to know we were seeing each other. Thought that might make his supervision of the project more difficult, might divide the team if they thought he was playing favorites. His request seemed reasonable at the time."

"So you quit."

"I was two weeks away from the end of my commitment period, anyway. I put in the remaining time and didn't renew. No way was I staying there after that. But I feel like such a dunce. And now I'm at loose ends—and back in Canyon Springs."

"Are you…intending to stay?"

Olivia ran a hand through her hair. "That was the original plan. I'd hoped to win my way back into Mom's and Dad's good graces. Gradually work into managing Singing Rock."

"Honey, I don't think—"

"That I can do it? Come on, Rey. You know I can. Paulette raked me over the coals last year, got me believing all the labels she's so generous in applying to me. Got me doubting myself. Which forced me to let Mom and Dad down."

"How many times do I have to tell you that you have to take Paulette with a grain of salt? She's always been sensitive to the fact that Mom and Dad gave us later kids more freedoms and opportunities than she was given. You in particular."

"So because she made the decision to marry right out of high school and start a family, she's jealous of me? You married your high school sweetheart and you're not green with envy."

"No, but you've gone to college, traveled all over. Been active in missions. You've done so many of the things she once dreamed of doing."

"You think because she feels that way and her husband doesn't want her taking over Singing Rock, that I shouldn't come back to manage it?"

"Do you really think it would make you happy? The hospitality part, sure. You're a natural. But what about the business end? That could make you miserable."

"Why? Because I'm the family's irresponsible little butterfly?" Olivia shifted impatiently on the porch swing, sending it rocking again, the chain supports creaking a comforting rhythm. She shouldn't expect them to understand. She didn't even understand it herself. All she wanted was to find the purpose God put her on earth for. She didn't want to miss it, so she kept stepping out into new things.

"I know you're frustrated trying to find your niche," Reyna soothed. Of the sisters, she'd been the most sympathetic to Olivia's situation. Must come with pastor's-wife territory.

"But what if that niche is right here in Canyon Springs, Rey? At Singing Rock. The whole time I was driving home that thought kept pressing on my spirit. That if I went home, I'd find the answers right in my own backyard. That it was time to step up to the plate for Mom and Dad and not let Paulette talk me out of it this time."

"We all know how much they've wanted one of us to take over their business, but—"

"I'll tell you how sure I am that coming home is the right thing to do. I got a call on the way here from Lanetta and Franki, wanting me to join them on a trip to the Holy Land. The Holy Land, Reyna! And I turned them down. Surely that tells you something about how strongly I feel about this."

"But they've hired Rob McGuire."

"I know." Olivia placed her foot on the porch, drawing the swing to an abrupt halt. "I guess I let them down one too many times. But I can make it up to them. I can—"

"I think he's going to be good for Singing Rock, Liv. You have no idea how hard it was for our folks to find someone with his background to come to a little town like this."

Olivia tapped her foot on the floor. Why'd the whole family think Rob was the answer to their prayers? They hardly knew him. "You don't need to sing his praises to me. I'm well aware of his knight-in-shining-armor qualities. I knew him in college."

"That's what I heard."

"And did your informant tell you Paulette told me to keep away from him?"

Reyna laughed. "I think I heard something along those lines via the sisterhood grapevine."

Olivia sighed. "Just because I don't lead men on when it becomes clear there's no depth of communication or shared beliefs and values, she acts like I'm a femme fatale."

"So what do you think of him?"

Her thoughts flew back in time. "He was a great guy. Friendly. Intelligent. Responsible. Hardworking. Faith-filled."

"One of those in-your-dreams sorts?"

"I suppose so," she hedged, sensing Reyna was on a fishing trip to find out where she stood with Rob. "But from what I've seen of him, it appears a few of those noble attributes may have rusted over time."

Compassion for one. He hadn't fooled her. His objections to giving the couple at Kit's a deal on a honeymoon cabin went far beyond the financial issues. He'd always held himself—and others—to high standards of moral behavior. Clearly he didn't think Aiden and Sally should be rewarded for an out-of-wedlock delivery and belated marital commitment. When did he become so unforgiving?

And what would be his verdict on her most recent

romantic fiasco? Would he see it as evidence, as Paulette most certainly would, of a frivolous nature? Lack of good judgment?

"Apparently he's had a rough go of it recently," Reyna noted, drawing her back from her wandering thoughts.

"Paulette told me." She started the swing going again, eager to move the conversation away from Rob. "And speaking of Paulette, is everything okay on the home front? I can't believe she has a job at Wyatt's. I didn't think she'd ever give up home-schooling and full-time homemaking."

"The family's had a few financial setbacks. Kids are in public school now. Except for Bobby, the kids aren't handling it well. Brandi's struggling. Rebellious. Skipping school."

Paulette's sixteen-year-old. The one the family teased for being an Olivia clone.

"So," her sister continued, "are you going to stick around or try spreading your wings again?"

Olivia stared across the clearing toward the lodge, at the light still glowing in the upstairs apartment. "With Mom and Dad leaving the place to a perfect stranger, it seems prudent to keep a close eye on things. Sounds like their new manager is cooking up so-called improvements for the property."

"That's why they hired him, Liv."

A shadow moved across the window and Olivia frowned. "Are things really that bad? Paulette alluded to it. And Rob flat out said it. Are Mom and Dad in danger of losing Singing Rock?"

"I would hope not. But that's where Rob comes in with his property management experience. M.B.A. His natural business savvy. They're counting on him. We all are."

"Sounds like you're essentially telling me the same thing Paulette did. Stay out of his way and don't interfere."

"Essentially? Yeah. I guess so."

The light in the upstairs window went out, leaving her feeling strangely empty. Alone.

Stay out of Rob's way? That might be an option for her sisters, but Olivia couldn't stand back and watch *him* turn their home into a cookie-cutter resort catering to people who needed to get in touch with themselves and God but chose instead to crank up the radio and drown out the still, small voice within.

Nor could she stand on the sidelines and allow him to cut her out of a future at Singing Rock. Or continue on his frowny-faced journey undeterred. The restoration of Rob McGuire now topped her priority list.

Doing the right thing. Rob shook his head Thursday morning as he rolled another coat of paint on the interior wall by Timberline's back door. What Olivia couldn't understand, with her lofty, self-righteous assessment, was that even if you knew what the right thing to do should be, it wasn't always within your grasp. It wasn't always *your* decision to make.

Like with Cassie. Angie's mom.

Or rather, her biological mother. "Mom" intimated a living, breathing connection. A relationship. Cassie didn't have a relationship with Angie. Didn't want one.

Didn't want one with him, either.

He dipped the roller in the paint tray once again. Then paused to gaze out the door at the forested surroundings. Already he'd come to appreciate the natural beauty of Canyon Springs. The quiet of Singing Rock. But in spite of a chilling encounter while inspecting homes in Vegas, one that sent him on a desperate hunt for a safer place to raise his daughter, it hadn't been an entirely easy decision to take the job. Despite his sister's assurance that small-town people made mistakes, too, were aware of each other's shortcomings—and failures—and made allowances for each other, he'd be giving up the anonymity a larger community provided.

When he'd started getting cold feet about the move, Meg said once townsfolk met his sweet Angie, saw how he was doing his best to make a home for her…well, they might shake their heads and cluck their tongues, but he'd find acceptance here. Desperate man that he was, he'd bought into that. Embraced that hope.

But he hadn't counted on the arrival of Olivia.

It was hard enough to admit to strangers that you'd fathered a child with a woman you weren't married to, and who wanted no part of you or your child. But locals hadn't known him before. Didn't know how at one time he'd set an example for others. Was a leader. Someone to look up to. To emulate.

Olivia was one of many who'd listened, rapt, when he'd taught undergrads at the Friday night Bible study on how to deal with having their faith challenged and values demeaned, or their beliefs mocked. He'd encouraged those young men and women to draw on God's strength, His faithfulness, to help them adhere to the moral compass they'd been called to follow on a lifelong journey.

A scoffing laugh escaped his lips as he again stroked the roller against the wall. Ironic, wasn't it, that not too many years later he veered off that very path. Way off. There was no doubt where he'd stand in Olivia's eyes once she learned of his no longer squeaky-clean past. He couldn't even redeem himself, make up for his poor judgment by doing "the right thing" as she'd no doubt see it.

"Rob? You in here?"

Grip tightening on the roller handle, he closed his eyes for a moment. Man, he hated to let her down. Hated for her to know who he really was.

"Yeah. Back here."

In a flash, Olivia joined him in the kitchen, waving

a handled carryout bag labeled *Camilla's Café.* "I thought you might appreciate breakfast."

Quite the turnabout from yesterday when she'd practically gotten in his face when he'd asked her to respect his managerial role. What was she up to? A cease-fire? He set the roller in the tray as his nose detected the mouthwatering scent of sausage and eggs. Hash browns. He could be bribed into a truce.

"Wow. Thanks. But you didn't need to go to all this trouble." The high-wattage smile she turned on him caught him off guard and, in spite of his suspicions, his frame of mind brightened. It wasn't easy to resist her friendly appeal. Her down-to-earth genuineness. Sincerity. And yes, those big brown eyes that drew him in, made his mouth go dry every time she looked at him. Maybe under other circumstances… but, no, he didn't intend to pursue a sure-fire rejection in the making. He'd already had enough of those to last him a lifetime.

"I was picking up something for myself, anyway." She peeled out of her jacket to reveal a form-fitting red fleece top, the color setting her smooth skin aglow. She shook the bag in playful enticement. "You like breakfast burritos?"

"Is Phoenix hot in June?"

"I take that as a yes." She grinned as she reached into the bag and pulled out a fat burrito wrapped in protective paper. Handed it to him.

He sat on a nearby chair, as eager as any kid,

watching as she placed paper plates, miniature containers of *pico de gallo* and a handful of napkins on the table next to him. Passed him a bottle of orange juice. Then she lowered herself to the floor, crosslegged, and leaned back against one of the cabinets to enjoy her own breakfast.

"Have you given any more thought to those Singing Rock upgrades?" She unrolled a chubby tortilla and added a healthy dollop of *pico* to the scrambled egg, sausage, cheddar and crisp hash brown mix. Rerolled it and took a dainty bite.

"Mmm." She closed her eyes, drifting off into a burrito-induced euphoric fog. Licked her lips.

He drew his lingering gaze away, endeavoring to focus on prepping his own breakfast banquet. "I'm still working on a plan. Mulling it over. Why? You have ideas?"

"As a matter of fact…" She reached into the back pocket of her jeans and pulled out a piece of folded steno paper. "I do have a few."

No point in ruffling her feathers. The least he could do after she'd gone to the trouble of filling his empty stomach was listen to what she had to say. "Let's hear 'em."

He bit into the burrito, the blend of ingredients melting in his mouth. Homemade tortilla. Fresh salsa. Good stuff.

"First off, forget the coffee shop." She squinted

one eye. "You said you weren't seriously considering that, anyway, right?"

With a shrug, he took another bite. Man, was this ever good.

"We could stock gourmet coffees in each cabin. Let people brew their own." She spread the paper on the floor in front of her. Took another bite of her burrito. Chewed. "And while I hate to do anything that would take away from the rustic atmosphere, I admit things look somewhat shabby. We could reupholster the furniture. Get new curtains. Linens. Give everything a fresh look. The cabins and the lodge."

He nodded, but noted her repeated use of the word "we."

"I have a graphic arts degree, so I know my way around some cool design software. Could help you revamp the brochure."

Picking up the bottled orange juice, Rob unscrewed the top. "Go on. I'm listening."

Dark eyes pinned him as she nibbled at the rolled tortilla. "I think we can come to a happy compromise, don't you?"

He choked on the sip of juice. "Compromise?"

"You know, on this upgrade thing."

"Sprucing things up is the tip of the iceberg of what your folks want me to look at, Olivia." He set the bottle down. "Singing Rock needs an entirely new business plan. Marketing. Image. Aggressively drawing new clientele. People who are looking for something that, as it stands now, this place doesn't offer."

She scrunched her face into a nevertheless engaging expression. "I don't think I like that word."

"What word?"

"Aggressive. It sounds hostile. Hard-line. That's not Canyon Springs. Not Singing Rock."

What else could he say to help her "get it"? He could understand why she was averse to a property makeover. Most people loathed change that forced them from their comfort zones. No doubt Singing Rock was her comfort zone. Home.

He made a placating gesture with his free hand. "Why don't you relax? Enjoy your vacation?"

"I'm not—" She clamped her lips shut. Shot him a guarded look.

He didn't know which was worse—the days back in college when she'd gazed at him in starry-eyed adoration or now when she unflaggingly questioned his judgment. "Trust me. I'm not going to turn this place into Disney World. But I have been hired to do a job. A job your parents believe I'm qualified to do. A job *I* know I'm fully capable of coming through on."

Why'd he keep harping on that? Was he trying to convince her—or himself?

Her brows rose in apparent surprise. "I'm not questioning your abilities, Rob. I'm merely concerned that the Singing Rock tradition may not be upheld."

"And that's where you come in?"

"We could be partners in this." She offered a coy smile, one that elevated his heart rate a notch. "Work together."

Partners.

Partners with a too-pretty female. Not a good idea. But if he let her think they were partners, wouldn't it be easier to keep tabs on her? Let her believe she played a role rather than squaring off in opposing corners like they had after she'd made the special offer to the couple at Kit's? As a partner, would she consult him before pulling another stunt like that— or think "partner" gave her the authority to do whatever she pleased?

His gaze lingered on her hopeful eyes. That much too appealing mouth. With a strength he wished he'd possessed years ago, he managed to focus again on his food. No, not partners. "I don't believe—"

"Don't think you can get rid of me so easily." Her teasing intonations caressed his ears.

His gaze jerked to hers.

"What makes you think I'm trying to get rid of you?" He cracked a smile. "I could get used to special delivery burrito breakfasts."

She stared at him a long moment, her smile faltering. Then she abruptly looked away, gathered her unfinished breakfast and stood. Disappointed eyes met his. A look he'd too often imagined the past few days. One he expected to see when she learned the truth about him.

"You don't take me seriously at all, do you, Rob?"

"Of course I do." He did, didn't he?

"No, you don't. You still think I'm one of your freshman groupies you can pat on the head and send on her way."

Where'd she get that idea?

"I don't think that at all, Olivia." Is that how she thought he was acting? Because of his attempt to keep some distance between them? "In fact, as soon as my ideas are solidified, you'll be the first to see them. How's that?"

She retrieved the Camilla's Café bag from the table, reached in and pulled out another burrito. Underhand-tossed it to him. He fumbled the catch, but managed to keep it from hitting the floor.

Avoiding his questioning gaze, she silently re-packed her breakfast items into the bag, then looped it over her arm. Picked up her jacket. Somber eyes once again met his, the impact of her disenchantment sending his spirits plummeting even further.

"In case you haven't noticed, Mr. McGuire." Her voice came softly. "I've grown up."

Hadn't noticed? Was she kidding?

Before he could respond in a way that wouldn't add fuel to the fire, she disappeared out the front door just as his cell phone rang. Baffled at her response to his attempt at a joke, he set aside his half-eaten breakfast. Stood. Should he chase after her? Find out what she thought he'd done to so offend her? She didn't think he'd noticed she'd grown up. Fat chance. How could *any* man not notice?

He started in the direction of the door, but the phone's insistent ring persisted and he jerked it from the clip on his belt. Better take the call. Let her cool off. Give him time to figure out what happened. How to make amends.

He raked a hand through his hair. "Singing Rock. Rob McGuire, manager, speaking."

"Don't you sound businesslike."

The familiar, lilting voice and accompanying giggle slammed into him with the force of a falling ponderosa.

His jaw tightened.

Cassie.

Chapter Seven

He hadn't heard from her in over a year.

Struggling to picture a woman he hadn't seen since Angie was six weeks old, he managed a steadying breath. "How's it going, Cass?"

"Fabulous. And you?" The voice that once upon a time charmed him now fell flatly on his ears, the intonations of a stranger. A nervous-sounding stranger.

He reached for the bottled juice. "I'm good."

"I got your message. That you'd left Vegas for Phoenix."

"Now I'm in a little mountain town called Canyon—"

"No, no. Don't tell me." He detected an abrupt change in her tone. Panic. "If I don't know, they can't get it out of me."

He tensed. Set the bottle down. "Who can't get what out of you?"

"My dad and stepmom." She paused as if having

second thoughts about the wisdom of the call, then plunged ahead. "I don't want to know where you are so I won't let that slip, too."

"Too?"

"I'm sorry, Rob. I didn't mean to say anything. But they tracked me down in California. Flew out from New York." Her words came quickly, tumbling in sharp succession. An avalanche. "We got into a big fight. So what's new, right? In the screaming match, I let it slip. About *her* existence."

A frigid wave surged through him. "And?"

"And I think they'll try to find you. Both of you."

He closed his eyes and drew in an uneven breath.

"It was an accident. I was so mad at them and they wouldn't shut up and kept at me and at me. I—" Tears choked her voice. "I didn't tell them your name. That's good, right? But I'm sure it's easy enough to find out. A matter of public record. I'm so sorry."

Her sob came clearly across the miles.

"You should have seen the look in their eyes, Rob, when I said 'baby.' They wanted to kill me. But I know them. When they have time to think about it, get over their anger, 'baby' will morph into *grand-baby* in their minds. They'll track you down. I know they will. You can't let them have her, Rob."

Her. She. Cassie never called her daughter by name.

"No chance of that." He gazed down at his free

hand, slowly opening and clenching. Opening and clenching. He had to call his mom. Warn her. Maybe bring Angie to Canyon Springs now, not wait until October when Paul and Rosa returned, when he'd be certain the job was his on a permanent basis.

"Do you remember how awful I said my life was with them after Mom died? How controlling they are? Manipulative. Nothing I ever did was right. I could never make them happy."

"I remember." Her parents had divorced when she was eight. Then her mom died when Cassie was barely into her teens and she'd been forced to live with her father and stepmother. She'd run away from home the first time at fifteen. Eluded them repeatedly until she was of legal age and they could no longer force her to return.

She sniffled. "I can't tell you how sorry I am. I cried all night. Gus is beside himself. He's never seen me like this."

Gus?

A sob echoed again. Crocodile tears? No, that wasn't fair. He shouldn't judge. "Take it easy, Cass. Everything will be okay."

It would be, wouldn't it? *Please, God.*

"They're used to getting whatever they want— them and those high-paid lawyers of theirs. But I swear I'll come and get her myself if you even consider turning her over to them."

"You know I won't." And God help the man or woman who tried to take Angie from him. "Trust me."

Another sob.

"Cassie? Did you hear me? I said you can trust me."

"I believe you."

"Good. Now settle down or you'll make yourself sick. You did the right thing in calling me."

"I'm sorry."

"I know you are." He could hear someone speaking in the background. A man.

"Look, I have to go now, Rob." Another sniffle. "Gus wants to go for a drive. Thinks it will take my mind off things."

Knowing Cassie as he did, she'd be but a mile down the road before her tears dried and the phone call faded from memory. Back in the moment. On to the next adventure.

How had he ever found that appealing?

With a heavy heart, he shut off the phone. He had calls to make. His lawyer. His mom. But he stood frozen to the cabin floor.

God, forgive me for being such a fool.

He'd said that prayer every day for three years. He knew God forgave. Had compassion on flawed, weak—stupid—human beings. But with the advent of Angie, his lapse in judgment wasn't something he could stuff in the closet, pretend didn't happen. Angie had been so tiny when her mother had taken flight. No amount of persuasion, pleading or prayer had gotten to her. She'd rejected her own child. Him.

God, please forgive me for being such an idiot— for hoping she'd eventually come around to wanting a place in Angie's life.

Deep inside he'd known the truth. She'd never pretended otherwise. But today's conversation confirmed, despite years of appeals to Heaven, that nothing had changed.

There was a dude named Gus to keep her occupied now.

With Cassie sounding a warning about her folks' intentions, she was free to move on with a clear conscience—without her daughter.

Close call. When he'd ignored her appeal to partner with him, she'd almost blurted out that she wasn't on vacation, but had returned home to manage Singing Rock. He'd find that laughable, wouldn't he? An inexperienced girl thinking she could manage a place like Singing Rock. But she shouldn't have said anything about his disregard of her, how he didn't think she'd grown up. That likely confirmed to him her childishness. Her immaturity. Her "little sis" status.

Olivia stared out a window at the late-afternoon sunshine filtering through the trees. She wasn't any threat to Rob's position. Not really. She was fooling herself. Even Reyna had been gently skeptical. The entire family stood by Rob—discouraged her from getting involved with Singing Rock management. So what was the point in staying in Canyon Springs? Maybe on the long drive home she'd made up the whole thing about sensing God's leading.

She sure didn't sense it now.

It would be easy enough to pick up the phone. Get in on the overseas trip. She'd always dreamed of going there, hadn't she?

Moreover, only days since the initial thrill of finding Rob McGuire right in the middle of her world, she had to admit that nothing would ever come of their renewed acquaintance. It wasn't a divine encounter, after all, nothing more than a coincidence. Not the stuff of storybook endings.

At least she didn't have to make a decision about what to do—whether to stay or leave—right this minute. That's one thing she *had* learned through the years. Step back. Let the emotion of the moment die down. Find a quiet place to spend time with God. Let His peace rule your heart and decisions.

But isn't that what she thought she'd done on the thousand-and-some-mile drive home?

The interior door between the lodge's main room and the office opened and a breathless, dark-haired teenager all but tumbled into the room, her eager gaze pouncing on Olivia.

"Brandi!" Olivia jumped to her feet and pulled her beautiful sixteen-year-old niece into a bear hug.

"Mom told me you were back, Aunt Olivia, but I had to come and see for myself." Brandi's hug tightened. "I've missed you so much."

"Same here." She held the teenager at arm's length, marveling at how sophisticated she appeared. Makeup expertly applied, shoulder-length hair casually tousled. Nails polished to perfection. A figure that must keep her poor dad standing guard at the front door to beat the boys off with a baseball bat. Olivia sure hadn't looked like that when *she* was sixteen.

"Don't tell me you drove here all by yourself."

The girl waved a set of car keys. "I've got my license officially so I'm licensed to drive on my own now, but no passengers except for family."

Before Olivia could evoke a promise to drive safely, Brandi grabbed her arm. "Is it true? I overheard Mom tell Aunt Lara you went to college with Rob McGuire."

"I did."

Brandi squealed, her grip tightening as she hopped up and down on tennis shoe-clad toes. "Did you go out with him? Is he a good kisser?"

Olivia laughed. "No and no. Wait. That's not entirely true. I have no idea if he's a good kisser."

"I'm sure he is."

"Probably."

They both laughed and Olivia's heart warmed. She and Brandi had long been on the same wavelength— both high-spirited, full of life, adventuresome. Which drove Paulette insane.

Brandi wagged a finger at her. "You gotta promise to tell me when you find out."

As appealing as that sounded, little did Brandi know that she and Rob *weren't* on the same wavelength. Far from it.

Brandi dropped to a nearby chair. "So tell me everything. What was he like in college?"

"Do I sense a crush here?"

"You can't convince me you didn't have one."

"Guilty as charged." Olivia laughed again. "But he didn't even know I was alive."

"I'm sure he knows you're alive now." Brandi's knowing look defied her youthfulness. "But come on, spill it."

"Okay, let's see, what was he like then?" She let her memory fly back seven years. "Snowboarder. Mountain biker. Guitar player. But what I remember most is how he was so in tune with God. Knew so much about the Bible. Had a gift for encouraging. For making those of us in the college-age church group determined to go deeper with God and raise our personal standards of conduct. To ask ourselves in every situation 'What would Jesus do?'"

"WWJD. Wow. A God guy. Those sure aren't easy to find these days."

"No, they aren't." She should know. "But never settle for anything less, Brandi."

"I won't." Her niece bent to fiddle with her shoe string, then straightened and motioned to the desk. "Where's Brett? And Elmo? Isn't this their shift?"

"Brett went to town, hoping to check Elmo out of the animal hospital."

Brandi's brows lowered. "He's...sick?"

"Injured. We don't know what he did to himself, but he got banged up bad. May have been hit by a car Tuesday night."

"He'll be okay, won't he?"

"Cuts and severe bruising, but the vet assures he'll make a full recovery." Olivia sat down on the edge of the office desk. Clasped her hands. "So how are *you?* How's school going?"

Brandi shrugged. Dare she mention Reyna told her there had been some school skipping? "I'm sure it's a big adjustment from homeschooling."

"It's okay." Another shrug. "I wish Dad wasn't on the road so much with his long-haul trucking. And that Grandma and Grandpa would come back. I miss them. Mom's such a bore."

"Things are still rocky between the two of you?"

"She can't get it that I'm growing up. Acts like I'm some ditzy kid."

Olivia's heart went out to her. She knew what it felt like to be labeled as frivolous and immature, all because you enjoyed life. Laughter. Fun. "I know it's hard, Brandi, but she's in a tough spot taking on a job outside the home after all these years. Prove through your actions that she's wrong. Focus on what God says about you, not on what others say. It's too easy to start believing things about yourself that aren't true."

"Whatever."

At the sound of a vehicle pulling up outside the office, Brandi glanced out the window, then leaped to her feet. "It's *him*. And he's heading this way."

"Him?"

"Rob."

Wonderful. How would he react to finding her here after their tiff earlier in the day?

Brandi smoothed down the hem of her T-shirt. Fluffed her hair. "How do I look?"

"Awesome."

"Good." She turned toward the exterior door with a dazzling smile just as it opened and the manager of Singing Rock stepped in. He paused uncertainly on the threshold, surprised to see the two of them, eyes focused on him.

"Have I interrupted something?"

Both shook their heads.

"Where's Brett?"

"Errands," Olivia supplied, amused that her ever-talkative niece stood to the side in rapt, wide-eyed silence. "Hopefully picking up Elmo. I'm covering for him."

Rob's forehead creased, and she detected a restless tension in his stance, in the fathomless grayness of his eyes. As if something was bothering him. Her, maybe? "He shouldn't dump his responsibilities on you. I'll have a talk with him."

"I volunteered. Don't worry. The place is in good hands. I grew up helping my folks in almost every aspect of running Singing Rock. Including this one."

"I'm not doubting that. I just—"

"Um, Aunt Olivia?" Brandi sent an adorable "excuse me" look in Rob's direction, diverting him from his determination to take Brett to task. "I need to run. Don't want Mom sending out a search party."

Olivia drew her close for a hug. "Thank you for stopping by. Let's get together. Lots. Okay?"

Brandi nodded, gave Rob a quick smile, then slipped past him and out the door.

"Paulette's kid, right?"

"Right. Brandi. Her oldest."

"She reminds me of you." He moved around behind the desk, seated himself and unlocked a drawer. "Family resemblance."

"So we've been told." She approached the desk with a hesitant step. "Are you taking over now? Or should I stay?"

"I do have things to attend to, but feel free to go if you need to."

Run along, little girl?

Ill at ease under his steady gaze, she nodded and moved toward the still-open door.

Then Rob cleared his throat. "Olivia?"

She paused, dread and curiosity mingling.

Chapter Eight

"About our earlier conversation—" Rob tapped a pen lightly on the desk, hoping a reassuring tone would ease the trepidation in Olivia's eyes. He didn't like knowing he was the source of that look. "I do respect your opinions. And there's no doubt in my mind you've matured since our college days."

Her faced flushed as if he'd told her she was the most beautiful woman on the planet. Which right at this moment, her smile widening and eyes sparkling, he could attest to.

"I apologize if I've given you the impression I discount your input. Your viewpoint."

She approached the desk. "And I'm sorry I took parts of our conversation too personally. There are a few things I'm probably too sensitive about—and people acting as if I'm still a kid, not a responsible adult, is one of them."

"I don't think of you as a kid. Far from it. But your oldest sister does, doesn't she?"

Her eyes widened.

Bingo. It was a stab in the dark but, in thinking over Paulette's asides about the unexpected return of her sister and speculation that she wouldn't stay long, he'd put the pieces together. Sibling rivalry.

"How did you know that?"

He quirked a smile. "Men can be intuitive, too, can't they?"

For a too-long moment they gazed at each other, guards down, then both grinned and spoke in unison. "Nawwww."

She laughed and Rob chuckled, the tension dissipating as if they'd crossed an invisible barrier. Better. Much better. In spite of all the things demanding his attention since Cassie's phone call, the falling-out with Olivia had disturbed him.

"I want you to know," he continued, a curious need to reassure her still driving him, "I'm not intentionally being secretive about my ideas for the property. I've only been here a couple of weeks. I'm still trying to learn the ropes. No time for anything else."

"I can free you up."

He studied her thoughtfully. He could use more help around here if he was to give attention to the business plan. Brett worked hard, but was part-time. And although a cleaning lady worked full-time, lived on the premises, there were things not getting done to his satisfaction. Things he'd had to assist with, which left little time to start mapping a plan. The days until Paul and Rosa returned were flying by, and he needed to get the apartment ready and a sitter lined up so Angie could join him.

Nevertheless, he shook his head. "Thanks for the offer, but you don't want this place eating up your holiday."

"I was thinking of staying longer."

Indecision flickered. "How much longer?"

"A week. Maybe two."

He didn't need her underfoot. A reminder of the past. And he certainly didn't need to catch himself looking forward to seeing her each day for the next several weeks. He couldn't deny the attraction, but that was asking for trouble.

"So what can I do?"

It wasn't a good idea, but the offer was one he couldn't afford to turn down. "This is the last big weekend of the season, and with Brett elsewhere for a few days I'm on my own. So I could use assistance keeping tabs on things around here."

"No problem. What can I do right now? This very minute?"

Her willing smile prodded at him, branded a guilty reprimand on his heart for planning to keep her occupied elsewhere. "Looks pretty much like we'll have a full house for the holiday weekend. Could you revisit the cabins that aren't yet occupied? Make sure everything's stocked. Kitchens. Bathrooms. Extra blankets and plenty of firewood for these cool mountain nights. Everything ready to go."

Her smile widened. "Roust out spiders taking up residence in the sinks or showers?"

She sounded as exacting as he was. This might work out, after all.

"Exactly." He returned her eager smile. "While check-in time isn't until three, we know guests will arrive before noon or shortly thereafter to see if they can get settled in early."

"And, of course, we'll accommodate that."

"Whenever it's feasible."

She nodded, apparently satisfied with his answer.

"I've been thinking, Rob—" She tilted her head, eyes shining. What did she have on her mind now? "How would you feel about an impromptu mixer for our guests tomorrow night? Nothing fancy. Hot dogs. Chips. Lemonade. Volleyball. Horseshoes."

"You want to throw a party?" He'd certainly consider special events on down the road, but there were no funds for something like that in the end-of-season budget. "We don't have time to pull it together."

She glanced at her watch. "Why not? I'll print fliers for guests at check-in. A run to town will take care of the food."

She looked so hopeful. Excited. He'd said he valued her input, hadn't he? If he said no, wouldn't that rob the sincerity from his words? Besides, loading her up with cabin inspections and a mixer to organize would maintain a healthy distance between them without seeming too obvious.

"I'm a party planner extraordinaire," she cajoled.

"Why doesn't that talent surprise me?"

"Guests will love something planned for the first night. It will break the ice. Let those who've been here before greet old acquaintances. Make new friends."

"You understand I don't have time to get involved, right? But if you think you can handle it on your own…"

She leaped to her feet. "I can."

"Wait, wait, hold on a minute." He did quick calculations in his head. Number of guests registered for the weekend. Approximate costs. "Can you can do it for a flat hundred bucks?"

It would be an out-of-pocket expense on his part, simply because he didn't want to disappoint her, but he couldn't spring for much more than that. Lawyers didn't come cheap.

"We have paper plates, napkins and utensils in the stockroom. So that leaves only food items."

He had to admire her gumption.

"One hundred dollars is the max," he warned again. "If you can do it within those limits, then have at it."

"Piece of cake. It will set the tone for the whole weekend that this is a fun place to be."

"Hope you're right." He smiled, marveling at her enthusiasm. "You'll still assist checking people in tomorrow so I can get some work done?"

"Sure. I'll go to town right now." She moved toward the door, then paused. "So Brett's not going to be around at all this weekend?"

Was Olivia taking a personal interest in that smooth-talking cowboy? The thought rankled, but he managed not to frown. "Helping at the High Country Equine Center. Horse events every day. That's right up his alley."

"Sounds fun."

A lot more fun than conducting spider checks. Was she having second thoughts? Thinking of joining Brett for a bit of high country horseplay?

"Better get to your party planning, Olivia. The clock is ticking."

She propped a hand on her hip, her chin lifting in sassy challenge. "You don't think I can do it, do you?"

"Did I say that?"

"No, but you thought it. Wait and see, Rob McGuire. Tomorrow night you'll be eating every one of your skeptical assumptions."

He grinned. "You don't say."

"I do say. And I expect you to show up for volleyball, too, mister. You got that?"

Out the door she went, leaving him to make a firm, but futile, attempt to extinguish a smile.

* * *

"You know, you *could* come out and meet your guests." Olivia poked her head in the office door for the third time early Friday evening. "Introduce yourself. Join in the fun."

As near as she could tell, everyone—except Rob—was having a good time. With Mom and Dad leaving the place to a manager who wasn't a family member, it would be reassuring for longtime guests to meet him. Get to know him. How many times did she have to tell him a huge part of Singing Rock's charm was its hospitality?

He didn't even look up from the papers spread out on the desk. "I'll be along soon."

"You said that thirty minutes ago."

"I'm saying it again."

She entered the room and sat down on the edge of his desk. "Is this your passive-aggressive way of giving the mixer a thumbs-down?"

"Of course not." Still gripping his pen, he looked up, eyes widening to see her perched there. "Activities are excellent promotional tools."

"I didn't do it as a promotional tool. I want guests to feel welcome. To know they're more than a credit card to us."

He tossed his pen to the desktop. "I'm just saying—"

She stood. "I hear what you're saying, and I won't bother you again."

He'd never make a go of this place with that

attitude. Then again, why was she so insistent that he join in? Her being the "face" of Singing Rock hospitality in her parents' absence would work to her advantage, wouldn't it? Olivia 1, Rob 0.

She'd given it considerable thought while inspecting the cabins. In spite of coming to an understanding of sorts with Rob, she still needed to find a way to win her parents over. To prove it was *her* guidance, *her* direction, *her* influence on Rob's decision-making that was the key to putting Singing Rock on the path to a bright future.

What was to prevent her from turning Rob McGuire into an unwitting mentor? Absorbing from him in the coming weeks everything she could about running the property from the business end? Then upon her parents' return, she'd make them an offer they couldn't refuse—to keep the property's management in the family and at a fraction of the cost at which they'd hired Rob.

Maybe that was God's answer—the leading he'd whispered in her ear on the drive home.

Two new teams of six players each were numbering off when Rob appeared at the edge of the sand lot. Oh, wow. Barefooted and dressed to play in baggy, below-the-knee Hawaiian print shorts, he looked like he meant business. A black tank top, showing off broad shoulders and impressive biceps, boldly proclaimed "I didn't come here to lose."

The slogan was met with masculine whoops and

applause—punctuated with giggles from a handful of teenage girls. Olivia's heart soared at the smile spreading across Rob's face as he was pulled in on the opposition's team.

"Everybody!" she shouted, unable to suppress a grin of triumph. "Meet Rob McGuire. Mom and Dad's new manager!"

Another cheer. Rob raised a muscled arm in acknowledgment, his glance snagging Olivia's. He winked, and her carefully thought out plans on how to unseat him from Singing Rock management wavered. What a smile.

Moments later they settled into formation and the game was on. Serves. Passes. Sets. Spikes. Blocks. Rallying back and forth across the net. Point. Rotating to new positions. Time flew for Olivia. Finding it much too fun to watch Rob play, it was hard to keep her eyes on the ball. His skills were too well-honed, too smooth, too powerful to have lain dormant these past seven years. Magic in motion.

"Oooph!" Olivia hit the sand on her belly. A dive gone awry, a missed attempt to halt a powerful game point spike from the other team.

From Rob McGuire to be exact.

He'd ducked under the net and now stood grinning down at her as his team gave a rousing cheer. She squinted up at him, still breathless. "You weren't joking with that shirt were you?"

He laughed as he pulled her to her feet. "No whining. We both played on the church team, so you know I take my volleyball seriously."

He released her hand and she brushed the sand off her T-shirt. "But we were on the same side back then."

"We were, weren't we? So, you ready to feed this hungry mob?" He nodded toward the fire pits as the players high-fived the opposing team. The sun had already dropped behind the tree tops, with sunset not far off. The night air would cool quickly, so hot food would soon hit the spot.

"I'm ready when you are."

He ran a hand through his sweat-dampened hair, then clapped his hands together. "Then let's do it."

Where'd he get this energy? Not stopping to catch his breath even at this thin-aired altitude. Definitely in better shape than she was. Volleyball had brought out his competitive spirit, too, the old Rob she remembered. He'd thrown himself wholeheartedly into the games—and now into the meal she'd orchestrated.

He headed off to check the fires and she ran inside for hotdogs and condiments. When she returned, several teenage girls had gathered around Rob, their admiring eyes following his every move. A shy smile here. A bold flirtatious one there. Boy, did that bring back memories of her Rob's Admiration Society days. Just as back then, Rob chatted with the girls in a friendly manner but never in such a way as to lead a girl on.

So unlike Kendal. The lying rat.

Amazingly, several of the teens she remembered from their childhood days. Regulars with their parents at Singing Rock each summer. She'd watched them grow up. And boy, had they grown up.

"Here you go, Rob." The covey of girls parted, allowing her to slip into their midst, all the while openly assessing her. Determining what her relationship might be with the handsome, athletic man. Determining if he was already spoken for. She'd give about anything to have an answer to that question herself.

As he distributed the hotdogs and roasting sticks to gathering guests, she placed a hand on his muscled arm to see if it would make the teenage girls' eyes narrow.

It did.

Had she once appeared as blatantly adolescent to him as these girls seemed to her now? So groupie-like, hanging on his every word, every glance? If he'd thought that of her, he'd never let on. She'd never caught him laughing behind her back, anyway. But then Rob was too much of a gentleman to bow to that type of behavior. With a such a stellar reputation and so many female admirers, how had he eluded marriage all these years?

He caught her puzzled gaze with an amused one

of his own, his eyes twinkling. So he *was* aware of the stir he'd caused among the young ladies this evening.

Before she could rib him with a clever line, a childish wail went up nearby. Olivia glimpsed a crying little girl, maybe two years old, pushing through the crowd. Obviously separated from her parents, the panic-lit face searched among the towering adults. But before Olivia could reach her, the toddler pushed past—to Rob. Hugged him around the leg.

"Daddy! Daddy!"

Startled, he stared dumbstruck at the tiny mite clinging to him. Then directly at Olivia, eyes dark with alarm.

She swiftly crouched, attempting to gently pry the child from his leg. "It's okay, sweetie. It's all right."

The red-faced toddler, lips quivering, stared up at Rob through tear-filled eyes. At last perceiving he wasn't who she thought he was, she screamed all the harder—which, fortunately, brought her real daddy running to the rescue.

Olivia rose to her feet as the parent-child combo reunited, noting with amusement that the teenage girls had scattered the moment the screaming started. Then she turned back to a still-stricken Rob.

"Whew." She laughingly bumped him with her elbow, addressing him with a provocative smile. "For a moment there, when the kid latched on to you and screamed 'Daddy,' I thought maybe there was something you hadn't shared with me."

Alarm again flashed through his eyes, followed by the now-customary frown.

How'd he get to be such a fuddy-duddy? She gave him an exasperated look and bumped him again. "Come on, Rob. It was a joke. You still have a sense of humor buried in there somewhere, don't you?"

Chapter Nine

Heart galloping, Rob managed a faint smile. "Yeah, sure."

"Then use it once in a while."

"Hey, I'm trying."

"Try harder."

She had no idea how hard he *was* trying. When that toddler plowed into him and he'd looked down, saw the brown curls, it was by God's grace that he didn't cry out "Angie!" A flashing second later, when he'd met Olivia's amused gaze, he'd realized the sobbing warmth that clung to his leg didn't belong to him.

But for a moment there...

Then came Olivia's attempt at a joke. Brushing it off left him reeling, almost as if he'd lied to her. But this crowd wasn't the time or place to break the news that he did have a child of his own.

"Earth to Rob."

He refocused on Olivia, who was watching him curiously.

"Yeah?"

"You okay? Those rounds of volleyball may have left you dehydrated. It's not that hot at this elevation, but the humidity is low. Sweat dries as fast as it forms, so people don't realize they're overheating. Don't drink enough liquids."

"I'll grab some water." He was such slime, letting her think overexertion was why he'd spaced out. It was a wonder, though, that he hadn't *passed* out. "You, uh, want anything?"

"No, I'm good."

He lingered a moment to take in the laughing, chatting guests gathering to roast hotdogs and marshmallows. With the sun setting, they'd timed the wrap-up of the games and commencement of dinnertime perfectly. Or rather, Olivia had. "Looks as if we've started the holiday weekend off with a bang. Thanks to you."

"And it looks like you've picked up a few new fans." She glanced mischievously in the direction of the flock of teenage girls huddled around a picnic table, their eyes trained on him.

His face warmed.

"That's mean of me to tease you, isn't it?" She arched a playful brow.

"You seem to get a kick out of it."

"I love to see a grown man blush."

A smile twitching, he shook his head and again

turned to find that water. Then paused once more. "Thanks, Olivia."

"For what?"

"For pushing me to get involved with the mixer."

"It *is* fun, isn't it?"

He massaged his shoulder. "I'll probably feel it in the morning. It's been a while. Out of shape."

"After the way you played tonight, I don't think anyone would buy that. But you do work too hard, Rob."

He shrugged. "You don't get anywhere sitting on your fanny."

"But all work and no play?"

"You sound like my mother." From the dismayed look on her face, that wasn't a comparison a pretty young woman wanted made. "Once the summer season comes to a close, life will settle down."

"Maybe. But you've changed, you know that?" She studied him as if trying to pinpoint the source of the problem. "You always had your eye on graduation and moving ahead in the business world, but you still managed to kick back, have a good time. I haven't seen much of that the past few days. It worries me. I'm not sure I like the Rob I'm seeing now."

She may as well have socked him in the stomach. If she didn't like what she saw now, she sure wouldn't like the rest of the story. "You sure know how to make a man feel good."

Alarm lit her eyes as she took a step closer. "I

didn't mean I don't like *you*. I mean, when I first met you, you seemed so balanced. In tune with God. I kind of expected you might opt out of the business world goals and head into ministry."

"Wouldn't qualify for that."

Her encouraging smile discounted his denial. "You were an incredible Bible teacher. You didn't let us get away with simply filling in the blanks of a generic collection of study questions. You made us dig deep. Challenged us. You knew so much about the Bible. About God."

"Knowing a lot about God and knowing God aren't always synonymous. And there's a difference between knowing what to do and doing it."

Olivia's smile wavered. "I don't mean I thought you were perfect. I mean there was something about you that opened up my eyes as to what God could do with a man. You set a standard."

He shifted uncomfortably.

"What I'm trying to say—and messing it all up— is you're so focused on work now. So serious. Never relaxing. Walling yourself off from people. That's not healthy."

He folded his arms. "You know, you've changed, too, Olivia."

Amusement again lit her features. "No more wild child? I can't believe the things I did back then. The dares I took."

"See? People do change. You did. I did. The difference is I like what I'm seeing in you, but you're not liking what you see in me."

She gave a huff of exasperation. "You're still not getting it. Here's an example. Yesterday Brett asked me 'does that guy ever smile?' Nobody would have asked that question in college."

"Come on, now, I'm not that bad."

"You don't think so? Do you know how thrilled I was to see you having fun during the volleyball games? Don't tell me you didn't feel the difference deep down inside you."

He had. It felt good.

"I like to have fun as much as the next guy. But life isn't all about fun. I'm not a college kid anymore. I have responsibilities."

"Everybody does. You're not unique. But back then you seemed to know where you were headed more than the rest of us did. Knew where God wanted you to go."

"Appearances can be deceiving."

"The corporate world wasn't 'it'?"

"Far from it."

She studied him with an intensity that made him squirm. What now?

"I understand you had a close call in Vegas."

Who'd told her that?

A familiar light sweat broke out above his lip. He wiped it away. "Wrong place at the wrong time."

"What happened?"

He didn't like talking about it, but the depths of concern in Olivia's eyes tugged at his heart. Maybe he could tell her. Some of it, anyway. He stepped to an ice chest and snagged a bottled water. Nodded to an empty picnic table set off from the others. She joined him there and he lowered himself to the bench across from her as twilight settled in, lending an aura of separation from the laughing, chatting crowd around them.

He unscrewed the bottle top. Took a long drink. Recapped it. Then sought Olivia's anxious gaze in the dimming light. "I'd left the job that originally took me there." No need to tell her he'd been fired. "Was doing home inspections that day in a mostly foreclosed neighborhood—where it turned out drug dealers had taken up residence in one of the empty houses."

She pressed a hand momentarily to her lips. "You stumbled in on them?"

"Yeah."

Had it only been a month and a half since he'd been shoved to the cement garage floor in that vacant suburban residence? The gritty surface scraping his cheek. Cold steel at his temple. Punches. Kicks. Threats as his captors rifled through his pockets. He could only think of Angie. His dear Angie. Prayed God would keep his little girl safe as she grew up without him. That she wouldn't forget him.

"How did you get away?"

By nothing short of a miracle. One of the men had found a photo of Angie in his wallet. Questioned if she was his daughter. He didn't answer. Didn't want them to know. Didn't want them trying to find her. Harming her.

His refusal to speak earned him another kick, but the first guy said he knew she was his—that she looked just like him. He'd jerked Rob to his feet, tied his hands behind his back with a discarded electrical cord and shoved him into the back floor of his own car. They drove for what seemed an eternity, Rob praying all the while for the safety of his daughter. That they weren't headed for home where the baby-sitter awaited his return.

When the car finally stopped, he'd been dragged into the blazing sun. Pushed to the side of the dirt road. In a haze of unreality, he'd known that was where it would end—with a bullet through his head. But to his shock, the man tossed his wallet in front of him. Said he had a daughter, too. Told Rob to go home to his.

"I'm sorry, Rob." Olivia's gentle voice, her touch on his hand, jerked him back to the present. Her eyes pooled with tears, as though he'd spoken his thoughts aloud. Had she read the trauma still reverberating through him? "I can tell this was a horrifying experience. I shouldn't have asked."

"No. It's okay. I probably need to talk about it."

He took another long drink, the cold water coursing down his parched throat, then set the bottle on the table in front of him, his hand still gripping it.

"They, uh, roughed me up—but good." He winced at the memory. "Took my cash. Stole my car. Then dumped me in the desert. I walked to a highway. Flagged down a motorist."

Compassion-filled eyes met his as she leaned across the table, hand outstretched to caress his still-healing cheek with the tips of her fingers. Caught off guard at the intimate gesture, he nevertheless held himself still, didn't jerk away.

"Thank God." Her whisper touched a chord deep inside, sent it reverberating, cracking the shell he'd so carefully built around his heart.

"Believe me," he managed, voice husky, "I do. Every day."

But why did he so much want to tell Olivia the truth of it? All of it. How he hadn't saved Angie— Angie had saved *him*.

Olivia had not-so-good news to share with Rob.

Still shaken from the ordeal he'd so obviously en-dured—clearly he'd shared with her only a superficial recounting of it—it was with mixed feelings that she'd heard the sound of his SUV pulling up in front of the lodge early Thursday morning. After a jam-packed Labor Day weekend, he'd hit the road—to wherever— Tuesday night. Personal business he'd said.

After seeing the raging emotion in the depths of his dark gray eyes when he'd shared with her his terrifying encounter, she hated to burden him with Singing Rock problems. She understood now how the near-death experience could have changed him. She needed to be sensitive to that. But as the man her parents put in charge, he needed to know of the latest maintenance issues.

She stepped to the open door of the Singing Rock office to find him, as expected, glued to a computer. This time at the office desktop, with Elmo curled up by his feet.

"Hey, Rob! Miss me?"

"Olivia. Good morning."

That wasn't an answer to her question, but would she want to hear him say no? The little pup, shoulder bandaged and tail wagging, rose and trotted over to her, limping slightly. She bent to pat him. "Good morning to you, too, little guy."

"I was glad to see he survived his ordeal."

"He's getting around pretty good." She stroked the pup's soft, dark coat and his tongue grazed her hand in appreciation. "Do you have a minute for me to fill you in on what's transpired in your absence?"

"Sure. I imagine you and Brett found plenty to keep you busy. Sorry I had to take off like that, but it couldn't be helped."

"No problem. We mostly assisted Mrs. Mabank with cabin cleanup in the wake of weekend guest departures."

"Big job. When I finish here, I'll lend a hand." He

glanced at his computer screen, obviously wanting to get back to it. "Anything else?"

Elmo bumped against her leg and she reached down to scratch him behind the ear. "Big monsoon came through yesterday afternoon. Left Sunflower's roof leaking—right over the bed. So I had to get the disgruntled couple moved to Creekside. Bigger cabin at no extra cost."

Rob groaned. Did he count that among the verboten freebies?

"Creekside was empty, so I figured it's better to keep paying guests happy."

"I have to agree," he said, much to her relief. "I'll get the roofers out there. Should have them check out all the cabins, anyway, before winter snows start piling up."

"Already placed the call. No rain in the forecast for the next few days. They can be out on Monday."

"Great. Thanks."

"I did find time to play with the brochure. I know you have ideas of your own, but I plan to take photos of the property while it still looks summery, then autumn and winter ones."

He pursed his lips thoughtfully, watching her stroke the pup's head. "Promoting Singing Rock year-round is something I've been thinking a lot about, too. Seems your folks haven't taken advantage of that as much as they could."

"There aren't as many people looking for a mountain cabin when there are several feet of snow on the ground. Not that it doesn't make a cozy retreat, but some years the road up from the Valley is treacherous. Even impassable, especially during times with few breaks between storm systems."

"Since we require a minimum two-night stay in the off-season and advance cancellation notice, people may be hesitant to book something they could get stuck footing the bill for."

She cupped Elmo's cute little face between her hands. "If the highway's closed, Mom and Dad don't hold people to that."

"Thoughtful, yet nevertheless lost income. But winter is a great time of year to visit. Seems we need to promote that more." He pushed back in his chair, a faint smile touching his lips. "You know, my folks took my brother and me up to Flagstaff to see my first snowfall when I was three. Loved it. One of my first memories."

"Which is probably what got you hooked on skiing and snowboarding. You did a lot of that in college."

"In the Flagstaff area, but I've never been in this region in the winter. I've always heard the Mogollon Rim, the White Mountains, get some of the biggest snows in the state. Guess I'll experience it firsthand this year. As I recall, you're into winter sports, too."

She laughed, warming to his relaxed demeanor. "Almost have to be, growing up here."

He tilted his head. Caught her eye. "Remember

that time the church group went to the Snowbowl? You were there."

Rob was reminiscing?

She'd skied. Rob snowboarded. But afterward they all met for après-ski time at an historic downtown eatery. She still recalled watching from inside the comfortable old building as fluffy flakes descended from lowering clouds. Could hear the fire crackling in the woodstove. Smell the cinnamon in her cocoa. Could still feel the thrill when Rob had sat down across from her at the bench-seated table.

"I recall taking a break," he went on, "and watching you come down the slope. I was impressed. You're good."

Rob watched her ski? "Thanks. You are, too. Better than good, in fact."

He nodded in acknowledgment, but to her disappointment he abruptly motioned to the computer. "Got a call from that young honeymooning couple from Kit's. They confirmed their October reservation. I entered it in the database."

Jerked from the jaunt down memory lane, Olivia cringed. Gave Elmo a final pat, then stood. Was Rob going to line her out on unauthorized giveaways again? Enough already. "Great. So did you have a good day off?"

His brows rose slightly, as if taken aback. But was that due to her sudden change in topic—or because he thought she guessed what he'd been up to on his day off?

"Yes, a nice day. Thanks for asking."

But he didn't elaborate. And avoided her gaze.

Which only served to increase her desire to get to the bottom of his reticence.

Chapter Ten

He couldn't keep Angie a secret from her forever. She was clearly curious about the reason for his absence, but too polite to ask. Would he tell her if she did—or continue to evade the questions in her eyes? It never seemed the right time to say something. And how did you segue into it during a conversation, anyway? Like during that chat about the cabin last week. *Thanks for calling the roofers, Olivia. And by the way—surprise—I have a daughter conceived out of wedlock.*

Rob grimaced as he tightened a bolt under the utility sink in the laundry facility. He'd talked to his lawyer. Alerted his parents to Cassie's warning. Nothing might come of it. Her dad and stepmom had little to no interest in Cassie as a child, so why take any in a granddaughter they hadn't, up until now, even heard of? But it was best to play it safe anytime you were dealing with moneyed people who couldn't make a move without legal counsel.

Still on his back, he wiped a grimy hand on an old rag. Maybe finding time to break it to Olivia wouldn't be so hard if she didn't constantly remind him how much she looked up to him in college. For pity's sake, she said he'd set a standard. He'd fooled her—and everyone else—into thinking he was something he wasn't. And the longer he let this deception go on, the more disappointed and angry she'd be.

He grimaced, and not for the first time considered holding off on bringing Angie to Canyon Springs. Waiting until Paul and Rosa returned, giving them two weeks' notice and disappearing out of Olivia's life before she learned the truth. Taking that route— the chicken's way out?—would address another issue, as well. Although she said he'd changed—even that she didn't care for the changes she'd seen in him— that didn't deter the sparks he sensed sizzling between them. A connection.

But it was a connection he couldn't pursue. Not once she discovered her hero had feet of clay. And it was still too fresh in his mind how it felt to be rejected by a woman you cared for.

He wouldn't willingly go there again.

Besides, no way would God trust him with Olivia. A fragile, beautiful flower coming into full bloom. Faithful. Trusting. Always hoping and believing the best of others. The man God had planned for her wouldn't be one with a track record like his, that was for sure.

He'd only break her heart.

"Rob?" Olivia's good-natured voice called through the open door. "There are some people here to see you."

With a shudder, he jerked upright, whacking his head on the bottom of the sink. *People? Cassie's parents? So soon?* Heart hammering, he rubbed his forehead. "Who are they? What do they want?"

"Roofers. For that leak at Sunflower."

He scowled as he got to his feet. "Why didn't you just say so?"

At the growl in his voice, she raised startled eyes to his. "I'm sorry."

"Never mind." He turned to lather his hands in the sink. Scrubbed them hard. Why'd she have to look so perky this morning, anyway? The bright blue of her cotton top set her skin aglow, made her dark eyes gleam.

"I said I was sorry."

"I heard you."

"Boy, somebody got up on the wrong side of the bed this morning."

"I have a lot on my mind." He tossed the hand towel to the sink, then brushed by her, all but stalking out to the roofing crew, nerves stretched tight. He thought he'd been handling things well regarding Cassie's folks. Taking precautions. Trusting God.

But snapping at Olivia showed how far from trusting he was.

She followed him out to the crew, listening in from what she probably perceived as a safe distance. Far enough away where he might be able to snap and snarl at her, but not get his hands around her throat.

He retrieved the keys to Sunflower from the office while she chatted with the workers, then he drove out to the cabin with them following. Olivia stayed behind.

He had to calm down, get a grip on himself.

He'd spoken with his lawyer about legal rights to Angie. About the evidence he had showing she'd been left in his care. As much as he was tempted to bolt when his employers returned to town, he'd assured his folks he'd bring Angie to Canyon Springs as soon as he confirmed daycare arrangements with a friend of Meg's. There was no point in his mom and dad being on guard, stressed out that Cassie's parents could show up on their doorstep.

The only time he didn't find himself on edge about that possibility was when Olivia popped in. Stayed to chat. She almost always left him smiling. But flashing red lights came with that, as well.

Leaving the roof to the work crew, he placed a call to Cassie on his way back to the lodge. He'd never seen a photo of her dad and stepmom. Had no idea what they looked like. To be on the safe side, he needed her to email one to him—and tell him their first names.

He slammed a fist on the steering wheel, a cloud of condemnation lowering. How could a man who'd called himself a Christian be in a relationship with a woman, father a child with her and not even know her parents' names?

His jaw tightened. Who was the man who'd carelessly allowed his spiritual center to erode over time, let it fall into such disrepair that he'd made one disastrous decision right after another?

He didn't recognize him. Never wanted to be him again.

Prayed to God he still *wasn't* him.

But Cassie didn't pick up on his call. Her phone wouldn't even let him leave a message. She—and *Gus*—were probably somewhere in the Australian outback by now.

He pulled the Jeep up in front of the Singing Rock lodge. Got out. Slammed the door hard enough to rock the vehicle.

"Rob?" Olivia's voice—tentative, cautious—greeted him. If he looked half as angry as he felt, it was a wonder she'd spoken to him at all.

"Yeah?" He approached where she waited by the lodge's main entrance, her eyes wary.

"I need to rearrange a few things in here. Make better use of the space. You have a few minutes to spare?"

Not really. He wasn't good company right now, either. But she couldn't move anything heavy by herself. The least he could do, after he'd been so cross with her, was help with the lifting. It would give him an opportunity to apologize, too.

Rob hadn't looked thrilled when she'd put him and Brett to work moving furniture in the spacious main room of the lodge. Grumbled a bit. It took some convincing to get him to see that furniture lined up around the perimeter of the room wasn't the best use of the space unless you were hosting a square dance. She'd gotten him to grudgingly acknowledge that over the holiday weekend guests had come in the door, looked around and left without lingering. Junked up with overdone cowboy-themed accessories and printed curtains that looked like they belonged in an eight-year-old's bedroom, it wasn't a welcoming setting for conversation and relaxation.

But by the time they finished and she'd shooed them out so she could add the finishing touches, he'd acted almost normal, his sense of humor surfacing. Now, ninety minutes later, Brett and Rob returned to see the finished product.

Standing just inside the doorway, Rob gave a low whistle.

"Amazing is right." Brett gazed around the room like a kid on Christmas morning.

It did look so much better now with everything rearranged—rugs placed to delineate cozy, conversational seating areas, and the more extreme accessories removed. She'd turned off the overhead fluorescent lights, allowing the tabletop lamps to lend a warm glow. A fire crackled in the stone fireplace.

Thrilled with the men's reaction, she waved them in. "Don't stand there, try it out. Make yourselves at home."

Brett headed straight for a sofa and flopped down with a satisfied grunt, but Rob quietly walked the outskirts of the room, taking in the details.

Bracing his hands behind his head, Brett grinned. "Gotta hand it to her, Rob. I think she's worked magic in here."

She watched Rob for a further sign of his reaction as he continued to slowly circle the space. Finally, he stopped at a leather chair and sank into its depths, his hands resting on its fat arms. Then he lifted his feet to the footstool on which she'd draped a patterned Navajo blanket, and settled his shoulders into the back of the chair.

"Well, say something," Brett prompted for her, apparently aware she was holding her breath.

Rob's eyes again drank in the expanse of the room, then met her gaze at last. "I like it."

Her spirits rocketed. "Told you, didn't I?"

"She did," Brett chimed in. "Made a believer out of me."

"Seriously, Olivia, what you've done here is remarkable." Rob settled more deeply into the chair, getting comfortable. "I can hardly believe it's the same room. I can't say I much liked the excessive cowboy culture clutter, but—"

"Come on, now." Brett frowned a reprimand. "Go easy on the cowboy stuff."

Olivia laughed, remembering the bronco and branding iron curtains. The thousand-and-one knick-knacks cluttering every available surface—horse-shoes and lariats, boots and spurs. She did keep the saddle-based lamp and select accessories. Just enough to keep the Western theme, but more under-stated.

A phone rang in the adjacent office and Brett leaped to his feet. "I'll get it."

Rob's gaze came to rest on the cheerful fire. "I have to hand it to you, this is nice. I think your folks will like it, and I know our guests will."

Our? "I'm glad you think so."

"You know, I wasn't too excited when you sug-gested partnering with me on Singing Rock projects."

She gave a scoffing laugh. "No kidding."

His forehead creased. "I was that obvious?"

"Let's just say I didn't have any doubts as to where you stood on the issue."

"But I think it may work out." Smile lines crinkled around the corners of his eyes. "You know, as long as I'm able to keep thinking up fantastic ideas like this—and you follow through on making them a reality."

Their gazes held and a happy warmth filled her. A smiling Rob was hard to resist.

"So you have more ideas like this one, do you, Mr. McGuire?"

"I'm sure I do."

As their shared laughter died down, Rob's gaze sobered and he eased out of the armchair. Came to stand beside her. "I'm sorry for snapping at you in the laundry room this morning, Olivia. You didn't deserve that."

She shrugged. "You said you had a lot on your mind. Anything I can do to help ease the burden?"

"Unfortunately, no. Business unrelated to Singing Rock."

Was the girlfriend trying to dump him? Had she *already* dumped him? He'd sure been mad about whatever it was, the way he'd slammed the Jeep's door.

"If there's anything I can do or if you need to talk about it, I'm available. Been told I'm a good listener."

"I appreciate that. You know, I was wondering—"

"What's going on here?" A female voice, almost a shriek, filled the room. "What have you done?"

Olivia stiffened at the sight of her oldest sister standing on the threshold. Hands on her hips, chin jutting, disbelief filled her eyes as she stepped farther into the space to stare at the made-over room.

"Where are the curtains I put up last spring?" She waved a hand, her voice more shrill by the second. "And the canteen collection? The branding irons and cowboy bobble heads? I haunted garage sales for months to find those."

Rob exchanged a look with Olivia. *Paulette had put this room together?*

"The public spaces needed some TLC." Olivia kept her tone level, soothing. "An inexpensive start toward Mom and Dad's intended upgrade."

Her sister's eyes narrowed. "You ran this by them?"

"I didn't realize moving things around for a more guest-friendly space called for parental approval."

"You should have asked them—or me—before doing something this drastic. How many times do I have to tell you to keep your nose out of Singing Rock business?"

"She ran it by me." Rob's voice, steady and sure, came to her rescue, halting Paulette's embarrassing tirade. "I gave her the go-ahead. Helped her pull it together."

Paulette swung toward him. "I didn't see this in your property plan."

Something unreadable flickered through his eyes. Rob had already shared his ideas with Paulette? Not her?

"The plan is still in the brainstorming stage."

"I didn't think you'd start doing anything until it was complete. Until Mom and Dad approved it."

Oh, boy, he was getting himself on her sister's bad side in an effort to defend her. Not a good idea. As always, Paulette would attempt to sway her folks' decisions. That would include the property plan—and whether or not they kept Rob on as manager. As much as she wanted to prove to her parents she could handle the job, Olivia couldn't let him flush himself down the drain defending her.

She stepped forward. "This was my idea. I bullied Rob into it. So if you have a problem with what you see, take it up with me, not him. But before you do, really look at it, okay? Put yourself in the shoes of a guest arriving for the weekend."

Her sister looked ready to pounce, but Olivia continued, not allowing her to get a word in. "Maybe they're reeling from a health crisis. Are a fragmented family in need of healing. A battle-scarred veteran or burned-out executive—all seeking peace, relaxation, restoration. Isn't that what Mom and Dad have always wanted Singing Rock to be? Not merely a business, but a soul-restoring retreat?"

"You think you can just waltz in here and start calling the shots, don't you? I thought we straightened this out the last time you were home."

Paulette's words came as no surprise as Olivia's memory flew to that fateful day last year when her oldest sister had ruthlessly undermined her self-confidence. Questioned her abilities and motives. Mocked her enthusiasm. She'd come home naively expecting the whole family to embrace her desire to settle down and help out at Singing Rock, but

Paulette had been adamantly opposed. Jealous, she now knew—and as Reyna confirmed—of Olivia's freedom to do so.

Humiliated, Olivia had caved and run.

But never again.

"I know you intended the cowboy paraphernalia to be fun and whimsical." Olivia's voice gentled, ashamed for Rob to be privy to this sister-sister dispute. "But I can't help but think you'll agree this room now better reflects Mom and Dad's vision for Singing Rock."

The flushed face and deeply V'd brows of her sister signaled an angry retort in the making.

"She's right, Paulette." Rob's firm words halted her. "Once you get used to it, I think you'll find it's what your folks told me they have in mind. Olivia and I are sorry we didn't consult you. We were both certain you and your parents would like it."

Paulette's jaw still stubbornly clenched, but her gaze again wandered to the soft lighting. Rugs artfully arranged. Pared-down accessories. Surely her sister could see the charm?

"What did you do with the old stuff?"

"It's in the storage building for the time being." Olivia glanced at Rob for confirmation. "We might be able to use some of it elsewhere. Maybe work it into some of the cabins."

The thought made her cringe, but she could compromise if that's what it took to restore Rob to her sister's good graces.

"Don't bother." Paulette headed out the door.

Olivia caught Rob's questioning gaze. Shrugged. Then hastily followed her sister onto the porch.

Please, Lord, don't let us part on a bad note.

"How's Brandi doing? She stopped by here last week."

Halfway down the stairs, her sister turned, still glowering. "She told me she'd seen you. She probably sang a sad song about how bad of a mother I am, didn't she? I don't know how Mom dealt with you all those years."

Olivia flinched. Paulette was still miffed at the lodge's makeover. That was all. "Maybe Brandi needs extra time and attention right now."

"That's something I don't have to spare." Paulette's chin jutted belligerently. "And don't go putting more ideas in her head. Since you got back, she's hauled travel guides home from the library. Has decided she needs to go to Europe the summer after graduation. Is badgering her dad and me to let her get a part-time job so she can save for it."

"Would that be so bad? It might give her something to look forward to. To work toward."

"You don't have kids and don't know anything about raising them, so don't start offering advice. She's sassy and headstrong enough without you encouraging that behavior. Cheering her on to chase off after wild dreams that have no substance."

"That's what you think I did? Chase after wild dreams?"

"Hello? Here you are, twenty-five years old. Finished college three years ago and you still don't know what you want to be when you grow up. When I was your age, I had two kids already. Another on the way."

Olivia's memory flew to what Reyna had shared—that Olivia had lived the dreams their oldest sister never had the opportunity to fulfill. But Paulette was wrong. She *did* know what she wanted—to be a wife and a mother. The very things Paulette already had in abundance.

She also wanted to be someone who practiced hospitality, who welcomed hurting people into her home. Helped them to know God in a deeper way. Encouraged them on a journey to healing. There wasn't a degree for that. No place to submit a résumé. No applications to fill out. No paychecks. That was just a part of her life. A part of who she was no matter where she lived, whether single or married.

But a loving partnership with a like-minded man, kids to love, a home to open to others—that was her deepest heart's desire. She didn't want to get married just to be married. She longed for a triune partnership with a God-chosen spouse and her Heavenly

Father. But until God chose to bring that person into her life…

"What I want to be when I grow up, Paulette, isn't defined by a paying job or my marital or parental status. It's not defined by where I live or how long I live there. It's defined by doing my best to cooperate with God's plan, trusting that He's working in me to grow and become the kind of person that will please Him."

Paulette dismissed her words with a deepening frown. "I can't let Brandi set her heart on unattainable goals, Olivia. If we let her work, it will be with the understanding she's saving toward tuition and expenses at a community college. Not for gallivanting off like you've always done. Are probably intending to do again."

"Travel is an education, too. You learn about other cultures. Other people. Yourself. God."

"Mom and Dad let you have your way on a lot of things that for Brandi's own good Vern and I can't cave on."

Meaning that they couldn't risk Brandi chasing after what they considered rainbows. Olivia would have to tread carefully if she hoped to support her niece in achieving her dreams. She'd told her she wanted to spend time with her, but a week and a half had passed and she hadn't once picked up the phone to call.

"Look, I've got to go," Paulette concluded. "I

stopped by to drop off a few things at the house for Mom. Please tell Rob I'll get back with him on his property plan."

Again, the hurtful reminder that Rob had shared his ideas with her sister and not her. All she could read into the days since her return to Canyon Springs was that nobody trusted her.

Not her parents. Not her siblings.

Not Rob.

Chapter Eleven

Rob kicked a fist-size stone and sent it sailing as sunset approached Thursday evening. He loved the still, quiet nights in the high country, but this one didn't have the usual makings for a customary sense of peace.

He *hadn't* shared his Singing Rock ideas with Paulette.

Not a one.

But she'd asserted she hadn't seen the rearrangement of the lodge in what she called his property plan. He hadn't even drafted a plan, let alone submitted one for her review. He'd promised Olivia she'd be the first to see his ideas, and from the wounded look on her face when Paulette made that comment, she remembered his promise, too. Which would reinforce her impression that he didn't take her seriously, didn't respect her opinions.

From the conversation he'd overheard between the

two sisters before he'd retreated to the office, his perceptions were renewed that Paulette harbored animosity toward her youngest sister. Judged her. Was much too hard on her. But Olivia hadn't lashed out at Paulette's criticism. She'd responded respectfully—and with a maturity and wisdom that caught him off guard. Maybe he'd misjudged Olivia a time or two himself.

"Rob!"

He glanced up to see a waving Olivia sitting on the steps of her parents' porch. His heart surged at the sight, but it was with acute reluctance that he diverted from his intended path and approached the house. He'd managed to keep one step ahead of her for days. While that hadn't kept him from thinking of her, wondering what she was up to, at least he'd stayed fairly focused on Singing Rock business. Found time to touch base with his sister about the availability of a sitter for Angie. Man, he missed his little girl. Daily phone calls and once-a-week visits didn't cut it.

Propping her elbows on her knees, Olivia cradled her face in her hands. "Sorry you had to hear that sister stuff the other day."

With her hair pulled back in a ponytail, he was reminded of the cute, lively freshman of his NAU days. A little too lively on occasion. Like when she'd accepted a dare to jump off a bridge on a missions trip. He'd been in charge of the spring break expedition and nearly went into cardiac arrest when he caught her making the leap. He'd chewed her out— and the guys involved—but that didn't make a dent in the daring gleam in her eyes. Thank goodness she seemed to have outgrown that phase.

He scuffed the toe of his work boot in the dirt. "Your sister gives you a hard time, doesn't she?"

"Understatement." Leaning slightly back, she rested her elbows on one of the steps behind her.

"My older brother does that to me, too. Thinks he has all the answers to things I never asked for his opinion on."

Her eyes brightened with interest. "Like what?"

"Oh, like he thought I should follow in his foot-steps and go into the military."

"Why didn't you?"

"Didn't want to get shot at, for one." He grinned, remembering the sometimes-heated brotherly alter-cations. "And I guess I had a stubborn streak in me, as well. The more he pushed, the harder I resisted."

She sat up, leaned forward. "So you have an older brother. Then the sister who married my cousin Joe is younger?"

"Right. It's Doug, me, Meg and Carly—the baby of the family."

"I doubt Carly appreciates that label. Paulette, ten years my senior, has used it against me ever since I hit my teens."

He propped a foot on the bottom step. "Unusual for

the oldest sibling to feel that way about the youngest. Usually the last-born charms the socks off the whole family. I can see you doing that."

She grimaced, either not recognizing—or choosing to ignore—his subtle compliment. "Paulette doesn't charm easily. But I notice you have her on your cheering squad. She seldom questions anything you do and tells me I shouldn't, either."

"Until the other day."

She shot him a discomfited look. "That's my fault. Thanks for stepping in front of the firing squad when she lit into me. Honestly, I had no idea she'd put up those hideous curtains or all that junk."

"A lesson for both of us—a good reminder that I need to communicate with her on a regular basis."

Olivia brushed at the cuff of her denim capris. "Mom and Dad didn't make her the manager. They picked you."

"Maybe so, but I get the impression when I'm around your sister that I'm auditioning for the role."

"I've spent most of my life auditioning for Paulette's approval. It's a no-win situation."

"Nevertheless, her opinion will carry considerable weight when your folks return. May determine if I'm a permanent fixture at Singing Rock or out the door come October."

"You know," Olivia's words came faintly and he strained to catch them, "my opinion will count, too."

And how would she cast her vote?

"I'm sure it will."

"I'm glad you agree." She got to her feet and pinned him with a forthright gaze. "Because I seem to remember *someone* telling me that when they had their plan for Singing Rock drafted, I'd be the first to see it."

"I don't have a property plan, Olivia. Only accumulated notes that I haven't shared with anyone."

Could he be telling the truth? He hadn't withheld his ideas from *her?* "If my sister hasn't seen it, then what was she talking about?"

"I don't know." He looked sincere enough, with his forehead crinkling up in that little boy look he sometimes had. "My laptop has a password, but I could easily have left my notebook on the desk. So if she stopped by when I'd stepped out, when no one was in the office…"

She wasn't buying it. "Why would you leave it out in the open where anyone could spy on your plans?"

He chuckled. "Contrary to your perceptions, I'm not trying to be secretive. Until I've sifted through concepts, weeded out the weaker ones and built a strong platform, I'm not much for sharing. That's all."

"But somehow Paulette got her hands on something." Her eyes narrowed. "How well do you know Brett?"

Rob leaned a hand on the steps' railing. "You think

he'd help her snoop? That kind of surprises me, considering how the two of you seemed to hit it off."

She reached up to secure the clasp that confined her ponytail and shrugged.

"But speaking of Brett…" He drew an ill-at-ease breath. "I'm picking up that he's on the rebound from a bad breakup."

Gossip? Rob wanted to gossip? It was all she could do not to laugh, but she managed to keep a straight face. "Who isn't these days?"

"What I mean is—" that deep breath again "—you're a pretty woman, Olivia. Full of life and energy."

Her heart skittered at the unexpected compliment. He thought she was pretty? She gave him an uncertain smile, hoping her face wasn't as crimson as the scoop-necked T-shirt she wore. But what did it have to do with Brett? "And?"

He glanced at the ground, his voice lowering, almost gruff. "And he might be drawn to that. You know, that energy. And life. And…prettiness."

There he went again with the flattery, but what was his point? "So you don't think I should hang out with Brett, is that what you're saying? Because he's recovering from a bad relationship and might be attracted to me?"

Like Paulette, did he think she'd stomp all over some poor guy's heart?

He nodded. Kicked at the step.

"Don't you think this might be a time when he could use an extra friend?" She couldn't count the number of guys and gals she'd been there for under similar circumstances. And them for her.

"I'm sure he can use…friends. What I'm getting at is—" He raked his hand through his hair and she could sense his increasing frustration. "I don't want you getting hurt. That's all."

He darted a quick look at her and she caught her breath. Was Rob finally noticing her? So much so that he might be jealous of Brett's attentions? Was he making sure she and Brett hadn't embarked on something behind the scenes that he was unaware of? Her spirits skyrocketed. Out with the old girlfriend, in with the new?

"Having at one time been your Bible study teacher," he continued, "I feel…protective."

Her throat constricted as her high-flying spirits dropped in a spiraling descent. He still thought her a kid. Thought of himself as her advisor. A disinterested guardian. Hopeful that in the dimming light he wouldn't perceive the effect his words had on her, she forced a smile and spoke with intentional nonchalance to camouflage the sting. "You're not my Bible study teacher now."

"I know that. But I feel obligated to give you a heads-up."

"Obligated."

"I mean, responsible."

"Responsible."

Rob gazed upward at the fading light, almost as if appealing to the heavens for assistance. Then he let out a gust of pent-up breath. "You're not making this easy on me, Olivia."

"I don't know what else to do because I don't know what you're getting at." Except that he wanted it clearly understood his concern wasn't personal. Not romantic. Just obligatory. Like a big brother looking out for his little sis.

Sheesh. How'd he let himself get dragged into this line of conversation? No, not exactly dragged. He'd instigated it himself. Had stupidly taken notice of how pretty she was sitting there on the steps.

Which led to this painfully ridiculous discussion, playing right into Olivia's sensitivity at being thought less than grown-up. But what was at the heart of his awkward attempt to counsel her? Concern that the overconfident cowboy might hurt her—or that Brett *wouldn't* break her heart, that they'd make a match?

He shoved the latter possibility aside. Cleared his throat. "I've said all I have to say on the subject."

"I should hope so." There was no missing that her cooling tones had become downright frigid.

What could he expect after coming across like some stuffy, authoritative elder? Not even with the advice of a friend.

He again scuffed a toe in the dirt. He shouldn't

stay, but he didn't like leaving on this awkward note. "I drove around the property a bit ago, made sure everything's secure."

She didn't so much as nod an acknowledgment that he'd spoken. Just looked at him.

"No incidents since last week."

Silence.

"So it looks as if our trespassers have headed back home with their parents."

"Brett thinks we should put up surveillance cameras. Hire someone to monitor them around the clock."

A muscle tightened in his jaw. He'd had enough talk of Brett for one night. "That would go over big with guests relaxing on their cabin porch. Or out for a romantic stroll among the pines."

He gritted his teeth. Why'd he have to say *romantic?* Anybody could go for a walk around here. Didn't have to have anything to do with romantic inclinations. Pretty women. Kissing. His gaze flitted to Olivia's inviting lips.

Get a grip, McGuire.

Determination renewed to not let her send him off with a cold shoulder. "Probably wouldn't hurt for Brett and me to take turns making the rounds throughout the night for a while."

"I could do that, too," she piped up, her gaze challenging. "After all, this is my parents' place."

He shook his head, not caring if she interpreted his refusal of her offer as a sign he didn't think of her as grown-up. "I don't want you out there prowling around alone. Even with high schoolers, you never know what they might do if they found a woman by herself. Or if they panicked at being discovered."

She squared her shoulders. "We could set a trap. Catch them coming or going."

"Too big of a property to conduct something of that magnitude. While there's one main entrance—and the road through the property circles back around to it—as you well know, there are other ways to access Singing Rock from forest service back roads. Hopefully we've seen the last of them."

"So you're confident it's kids? Not adults with criminal intent?"

"I'm hoping that's not the case."

"Not a pleasant prospect, especially after your experience in Las Vegas."

"No." He rubbed the telltale tension from his shoulder. He didn't want to talk about that. But while her tone held little of the warmth he'd come to expect of her, at least she was speaking to him.

Another long stretch of silence, but it was Olivia who broke it this time. "The Las Vegas area was hit hard when the bottom dropped out of the economy. So you were laid off? That's when you became a property inspector?"

He flashed her a quick, considering look. She'd figured that out? But it hadn't been your standard, across-the-board layoff as she assumed.

"Right. I'd been working in the financial department at a cutting-edge construction company. Nevada's so much more than a gambling capital. It was one of the fastest-growing areas in the country back then."

"And you liked it enough to stay there."

"Enough. I wanted to remain in the general area for a while, so I took a job with a friend who was master-certified as a home and commercial building inspector. Basically apprenticed with him. Started the process for my own certification."

"And then you came here…afterward."

He nodded. So much had happened in the time since he'd been fired and the day he'd arrived to interview in Canyon Springs. A lifetime's worth of choices. Some of them good, some not so good. But one that, in spite of his wrong choice, God used to bring him his greatest blessing. Angie.

"So what about you, Olivia?" He wanted to keep her talking. Ease further from that awkwardness he'd instigated. "What have you been doing since my infamous graduation day?"

She did smile at that, as he'd intended. "You know most of it, remember? From when we ate at Kit's?"

"Right, right." Lunch with Brett. How could he

forget? "Odd jobs, missions work. You said you liked what you called living out of a suitcase."

"It's fun. I love meeting new people. Seeing new places. Facing new challenges. But I love coming home. That's why—"

He strained to see her features as twilight descended into near-darkness. "Why what?"

"Why I came home. For a visit."

"So what's next? After the visit, I mean."

"A trip to Israel may be in the works."

A knot formed in his stomach. That was for the best, right? Get her out of town. "Sweet."

"Yeah, it is. The year after you left NAU, a group of girls from the church went during spring break. I couldn't swing it financially, but everyone said it was a deeply meaningful journey—even without Romeo Rob."

He caught the amusement in her voice. Heard the giggle.

"Excuse me?"

"That's what the girls in Bible study called you. Romeo Rob. Code word R.R."

He'd known of the fan club, but not that silly name. "You're kidding."

"Nope. And if you didn't know that, you probably didn't know why the Saturday night service was always packed when you led worship."

He wasn't sure he wanted to know. He didn't like

thinking about his college days. To remember how far he'd fallen.

"They came to see you. I mean, the girls did, anyway."

"That's supposed to make me feel good? That I distracted young ladies from worship?" Things were worse back then than he'd thought.

"No, no. Not a distraction. An inspiration. It was your connection to God that made you so appealing. You may not be aware of it, but godly guys are few and far between."

"I wasn't any more godly than your average guy." Far from it.

"Are you kidding? You actually *read* your Bible. And when you prayed, it was like you were talking to your best friend sitting right next to you. You were open, transparent, about your struggles to live a Christian life. Women want more than a Sunday morning male, Rob. It's a good thing to be a man recognized and admired for his godly character."

Renewed shame filled him. The more she hammered home who she thought he'd been, the less he believed he could ever become such a man.

He should tell her right now. Get it over with. Put a halt to her starry-eyed hero worship. He took a shaky breath. *Please, God, give me the right words. And please don't let her hate me.*

She lightly touched his arm. "I promised my sister

Claire I'd call at seven. It's just a few minutes 'til. Guess I'll see you tomorrow."

"Yeah. Sure." Guilt mingled with relief—and resolve.

Tomorrow.

He'd tell her tomorrow.

Chapter Twelve

"You look like gloom and doom this morning."

And he did. Mr. Frowny Face was back in full force. Hair roughed up and shoulders hunched over the computer keyboard, he looked like he could use a shave—although Olivia kind of liked his unkempt appearance.

Brett, relaxed in a nearby chair and toying with the Western hat in his hands, chuckled. Whatever had Rob riled up hadn't fazed him. Then again, little seemed to bother the good-natured guy.

"Our luck ran out." Rob pushed back from his desk. "Ramblewood had a visitor in the night. Apparently they couldn't get in, didn't break any windows, but they spray-painted the front door. Same 'no more' message. Knocked over flower pots on the porch."

"So it wasn't those kids, after all." She'd hoped for all their sakes this episode was over with summer's end.

"At least not out-of-towners."

"So what do we do now?"

"I notified the county sheriff's department, just to get it on record. Photographed it like you did at Bristlecone."

"Not much the county can do though, right? But what can we do?"

"Patrol. We may not be able to catch them, but maybe we can make it uncomfortable enough with frequent passes through the property to ward them off. May have to look into those security cameras Brett mentioned."

Brett leaned forward. "What we need is a tower, the kind the forest service mans to watch for fires."

Olivia turned toward him. "You know, if you get up on that rocky ridge to the west of here, the one you can see from Hummingbird, you can get fairly high up. Can't see all the cabins, of course, but in the dark you'd detect lights through the trees in the more far-flung areas. Those are the ones that seem to be targeted—because they're more remote."

"That might not be a bad idea. One—or *two*—of us up there on lookout." Brett shot Olivia a meaningful look, his grin suggesting this might be fun. "Another stationed below, back in the trees. Waiting for a call to move in."

"I can show you how to get up there. It's kind of a climb. We'd need to go before it got dark."

Rob stood, as if taking command. "Let's not go jumping the gun here. We need to think this through."

A still-grinning Brett winked at Olivia.

Rob's brow lowered. "You have something you want to say, Marden?"

"Not a word." But a smile still tugged as he cut Olivia a conspiratorial look.

Rob looked from one to the other. All but glowering. This vandalism thing must really be getting on his nerves.

"You know, I can leave the room if you two have something that needs to be discussed in private."

"Not necessary." Brett rose to his feet and moved toward the door. "Just let me know when you have it all worked out. What you want me to do. When and where, and I'll report for duty."

He tipped his hat with another smile and made his escape. Rob moved to the door, watched him on his way, then turned back to Olivia, who quickly suppressed her own smile.

Olivia was the most stubborn little thing he'd ever encountered. He didn't want her sitting up on some ledge all night with Brett—or parked down below in his pickup truck—and he suspected she knew it. "So where is this lookout?"

"It's actually on forest service property. It's been years since I've been up there, but I think I still know the way. It's my second most favorite place to go for a quiet time."

"And the first?" He couldn't help asking, stupidly wanting to know more about Olivia.

"The footbridge over the creek. Easier to get to."

He nodded and ran his hand through his hair. "I'm thinking we can put Brett down here at ground zero. I'm not keen on anyone 'moving in' as he suggested, though. I think we have pranksters, not a hardened criminal element, but I wouldn't want to take any chances."

"You mean if they're armed?"

"Right. But someone will need to show county law enforcement the way back in there. We need to make sure our vandalizing varmints are caught on Singing Rock property, in the act if at all possible."

"We can park the Jeep at the base of the lookout. It's out of the way. Nobody will see it."

We? Guilt gnawed to tell her about Angie, but he sure couldn't risk it tonight or she might start yelling at him and spook off their prey—or draw armed trespassers to their isolated location. But now wasn't the time or place for a "big reveal" either. Brett could return any moment.

"I really don't want you involved in this at all, Olivia. You can show me how to get up there and that's it."

"Then it looks like you'll have to find your own way."

"Come on. Climbing up there at night wouldn't be safe. That's why I'm volunteering instead of asking Brett to do it."

"We won't be climbing at night. We'll go up before dark."

"*We* are not going to do any such thing."

"Very well." She smiled up at him sweetly. "Then I'll be down below—with Brett. And you can find your own way." She glanced at her watch. "You may want to get started now. The route isn't marked. Not easy to find."

"Cold?"

"Some." Olivia scooted farther back on the ledge to lean against the rock outcropping behind them, sheltering herself from the steady breeze that was so common in the mountain country. Usually the wind died down at night, but not this evening. Or rather, not at this time of morning. Two o'clock.

Rob scooted back, too, his arm brushing comfortably against hers. Then to her surprise, he lifted his hand and touched her lightly on the cheek, the back of his fingers warming her chilled skin. "You *are* cold. You want my jacket?"

"I'm okay." The shiver that preceded her comment had little to do with the cooling temperature. "But thanks."

Already snuggled down in her own sweatshirt and windbreaker, she didn't need to stake a claim to his. But the thought of nestling into a Rob-warmed jacket had its appeal.

"You sure? We can go back. Looks like our uninvited guests intend to be no-shows tonight."

"I'm fine." *But if you touch me one more time, I won't be held responsible for my actions.* Throughout the long night watch, it was all she could do to keep her attention on scouting out trespassers in the dim landscape stretching below them. Curb thoughts from wandering to her niece's intriguing question... *is he a good kisser?*

They'd talked quite a bit off and on about the vandalism. And other things. Sometimes with extended periods of comfortable silence. She'd shared stories of growing up in Canyon Springs. He, about his own youth. Both about how much they loved their families. Were blessed to have had such wonderful ones when so many they knew didn't share that experience.

Conversation lulled again as she scanned the landscape with binoculars, still acutely aware of Rob's proximity. Then she sat up straighter, pointed into the gray-washed night. "Look. There. I saw movement. Off to the left. Where you can glimpse the road curving, not far from Juniper."

She handed the binoculars to Rob and he inspected the area she'd drawn his attention to. "Looks like a coyote."

Disappointed, she leaned against the rocky surface once more. She wanted to spot the bad guys tonight, once and for all. Phone down to Brett to move in for a closer look. Call the county sheriff's department if prowlers were confirmed. "At least it's not a mountain lion. Or a bear. We have those around here, too, you know."

"So I've heard."

Rob set aside the binoculars and settled in to wait once more, his arm again resting against hers as she studied his strong profile in the starlight that turned the world to black and white. He pulled his knees up where he could rest his forearms on them. "Quite a night, isn't it? I don't think I've ever seen the Milky Way jump out like that."

"You're a mile closer to it than most people in this country are. Makes a big difference. Mom and Dad used to bring us up here to stargaze when we were kids."

It was family fun back then. But tonight the stars spelled out r-o-m-a-n-c-e. Was it just her, or did Rob feel it, too?

"Incredible view of Singing Rock," he went on. "Hammers home how big the property and the surrounding forest are. Brett may be right about hiring security. We can't sit out here every night on the off chance someone shows up."

Hadn't they already talked enough about prowlers and property protection for one night?

"Oh, I don't know about that." She looped her arm through his and leaned into him, absorbing his warmth as she whispered into his ear. "Isn't it a whole lot more fun sitting here in the dark with me than chatting with boring old security guards?"

She heard the soft catch of his breath as he turned to her, his face mere inches from her own. So close. So kissing close. Heart hammering, she mentally kicked herself as the charged moments ticked by. Why'd she always say the first stupid thing that popped into her head?

Unwillingly, she loosened her grip, started to slip her arm from his, but his strong hand stayed her. And she froze.

"Guess it does have its perks, now doesn't it?" The husky words caught her off guard.

She swallowed, her breathing as uneven as a wind-roughened lake. "It does."

"You know what I remember most about you from college?"

He was finally getting around to reminiscing about the good old days? Right now?

"You never noticed me in college, Rob McGuire." She held herself still, conscious of a chord of awareness vibrating between them as he gradually leaned in closer.

"But I'm noticing you…now."

She wet her lips. "You are?"

"Yeah. Yeah, I am."

"I'm noticing you, too." She took a quivering breath. "But then, I've always noticed *you*. I mean—"

He put a warm, silencing finger to her lips. "You're a very special woman, Olivia."

Mouth suddenly dry, she couldn't have responded if her life depended on it.

"I don't think you know quite how special." He paused, his fingers brushing the hand that still gripped his arm. "You're good company."

Her shoulder slumped into his. "Like one of the good old boys down at the local sports bar?"

He chuckled softly. "No. I don't think there's a man alive who would make that comparison. What I mean is—I enjoy spending time with you."

"You could have fooled me. I mean, after all—"

He once again placed his finger momentarily to her lips, his voice almost gruff. "Hush, Olivia."

She stilled.

He leaned in. Hesitated. Then captured her mouth with his.

Chapter Thirteen

You had no business kissing Olivia Diaz.

The condemning voice roasted him on a spit of self-condemnation hours after they'd left their perch overlooking Singing Rock. Long after they'd carefully climbed down the flashlight-lit trail to the base of the overlook. Walked hand in hand to the Jeep.

Even this morning, as daylight crept through the wooden slats of his bedroom blinds, he could still taste the sweetness of her lips. Feel her soft face cupped in his hand. Smell the citrus scent of her hair. Touching his lips to hers had seemed so inevitable. So good. So right.

But there had been another time in his life when something felt right—and was so wrong.

He squeezed his eyes shut. He hadn't kissed Olivia carelessly or without meaning, but this morning reality slammed him into the wall. He'd kissed her—encouraged and accepted her kisses in return—and yet he hadn't confessed the truth about Angie. About Cassie. For days he'd intended to find the right time and place. The right words. Was that why he'd given in and kissed her last night? Knowing that once she knew the truth about him, there would be no more kisses? No more hope that she could come to care for a man carrying the burden of a less-than-heroic past?

Sitting there talking to her for hours last night… sharing memories and laughter with her cuddled up against him, he couldn't help but be further drawn to the woman Olivia had become. Or think about what it would be like to share a life that included both her and his Angie.

He slammed his fist into the pillow on which he hadn't gotten a wink of sleep. It had almost killed him to tell his parents, but this was far worse. He hadn't respected Olivia enough to tell her, to let her make an informed decision as to whether or not to kiss him back. He couldn't pretend he didn't know the type of man she trusted God for. Couldn't act as if he had no idea who she believed him to be. For all intents and purposes, he'd taken advantage of the moment when it presented itself last night. Taken advantage of Olivia.

But he'd tell her today.

He threw back the covers and sat up in bed. He couldn't live with a lie one moment longer. It wasn't fair to let Olivia believe in a man who didn't exist—except in her dreams.

Rob McGuire.

Olivia's giddy heart sang his name over and over as she showered and dressed for the day, taking extra care with her hair and makeup. Carefully selecting her newest pair of jeans. A cute, red-and-black silky top. Silver hoop earrings. She didn't even feel the lack of sleep.

Rob—Romeo Rob—had kissed her. Or had she dreamed it?

She spun in front of the bedroom's full-length mirror, checking out her choice of outfits. No, she hadn't dreamed it. She could still feel his lips gently, insistently, moving on hers. Feel his fingers clasped with hers as he walked her to her parents' door. Remember how he'd kissed her again on the front porch.

After seven long years, never supposing she'd ever run into Rob again, the crush she'd harbored in college had blossomed, renewed into something more than she could ever have imagined.

Thank you, God.

She peeked out the lacy-curtained window toward the lodge. Singing Rock's vehicles and Rob's own SUV sat to the office-side of the building, next to one of the big ponderosas. So he hadn't gone anywhere yet this morning. With a last look in the mirror, she hurried downstairs and dashed out the door.

When she stepped into the office, disappointment assailed her at finding Rob's assistant rather than the manager himself. But she spied his laptop case and cell phone sitting on the credenza, so he couldn't be too far away. "Morning, Brett."

"Now don't you look prettier than a rose in spring." Brett's appreciative once-over left her hoping Rob would echo his assistant's approbation.

"Thanks. Rob around?"

"He walked down to River Rock. Something about a blown fuse. Shouldn't take too long."

She nodded and moved to peek out a window. Should she hang out? Wait for him? Or come back later? "Things quiet here this morning?"

"Got a couple of calls asking when aspen colors are expected to peak. What the highs and lows are this time of year. Booked a cabin."

"That's good." She turned toward him, only to find him pushed back in his chair, hands clasped on his flat stomach—grinning at her.

"What?"

"You tell me."

Her face warmed. "Nothing to tell."

"Is McGuire treating you all right?"

"Why wouldn't he?"

Brett shrugged, his smile lingering. "Just checking. Sometimes I get the impression he's oblivious to what's going on around him. You know, right under his nose. Like a pretty lady trying to get his attention."

She laughed. Was she that obvious? "You can stop your worrying, Brett. His attention's been caught."

"About time. But if things don't work out, you know where to come."

She shot him a guarded look, remembering what Rob had told her about Brett's misfortune in the romance department. How he might be looking for a replacement—and that Olivia might fit the ticket. She laughed again. "I'll keep that in mind."

"Excuse me," a cheery voice called out from the open doorway, followed by a gray-haired head topping a rotund body. "I need to run into town, but my car won't start. It may need to be jumped. Anyone in here know the tricks?"

"That would be me, ma'am." Brett rose, settling his Western hat on his head.

"I'll cover the phones for you." That gave her a good excuse to wait for Rob.

From the look on Brett's face, he saw right through her ploy. He tipped his hat, winked and disappeared out the door, pulling it shut behind him.

She peered out the window again, but no sign of Rob. She moseyed restlessly around the room. Organized the pen and pencil cup. Checked the desktop computer for email queries. Straightened Rob's laptop case. His cell phone.

She'd barely touched it when it rang. Rang again.

Oh, well. "Rob McGuire, Singing Rock. Olivia speaking."

"May I speak to Rob, please?" The tense voice of a woman. "This is an emergency."

Olivia's stomach jolted. "He stepped out of the office for a short while. May I get a message to him?"

"This is his mother. Angie's been hospitalized."

Angie?

"An allergic reaction to a bee sting. The doctors think she'll be okay. But they're talking about keeping her overnight for observation. There's a danger of bacterial infection."

"That sounds serious."

"Have Rob call me, please. He has my number."

"I'll find him immediately."

"Thank you. She's the love of my son's life."

The line went dead.

The love of Rob's life. With trembling fingers, she shut off the cell phone, crossed the room, then jerked open the door. Plowed straight into Rob.

Laughing, he caught her in his arms. "Hey, what's the hurry? Train to catch?"

"Your mom called." Her words came in a breathless rush. "She said to tell you Angie's been hospitalized."

His smile froze. Still gripping her arms, his eyes searched hers.

"A bee sting. They're keeping her for observation."

She forced the cell phone into his hands. "You're supposed to call your mom."

He clutched the phone and brushed by her, speed dialing as she followed him into the main room of the lodge. Without a word, he took off up the stairs to his apartment, two at a time.

Heart racing, Olivia stared after him. Who was this mystery woman? The girlfriend she'd feared for weeks? Until last night. Until he'd kissed her and put her fears to rest.

From above, drawers and doors opened. Slammed. She could hear his muffled voice as he talked to his mother. Terse. Concerned. Then he appeared again, dashing down the stairs, duffle bag in hand.

"Is there anything I can do to help, Rob?"

He jerked to a halt, as if stunned to still find her standing at the bottom of the staircase. "If you could watch over things until I get back. I—"

He seemed at a loss for further words.

"I can do that. Don't worry. I'll handle it."

"Thanks."

She followed him into the office where he snagged his computer case and hoisted the strap over his shoulder.

"Is everything going to be okay? It sounded serious."

He avoided her gaze. "Mom says she's resting comfortably. Asking for me. So I need to get down there."

"I don't remember you mentioning a family member named Angie." She may as well hear it now. Stop living in a dream world if Rob's heart was already spoken for. "Your mom called her the love of your life."

His eyes clouded. "She is."

"And she's your—?" Friend? *Girl*friend? "I don't recall—"

He held up a restraining hand. "Olivia. Stop."

Staring into his eyes, she saw the torment. Indecision.

"Mom didn't tell you? Angie—" He drew a ragged breath, eyes boring into hers. "Angie is my daughter. My two-year-old daughter."

She stared at him, not comprehending. Then, as if picked up and slammed to the ground, realization dawned. *Another married man?* Hot humiliation boiled over, igniting nerves throughout her body. "I—I didn't know. You don't have a ring. Why didn't you tell me? I mean you even—"

Kissed me.

"I'm not married, Olivia."

Her eyes questioned as she struggled to understand.

"I'm not divorced." He dragged his gaze from hers to stare at the floor. "I've never been married."

"I don't understand."

She lightly touched his arm and he looked at her again, resolve in his tone. "Angie is my daughter from a previous relationship. No marriage. No divorce. No wife. No ex-wife. Only a child I love more than life itself."

She swallowed, hearing but still not comprehending.

"Look, I'm sorry, Olivia. This is not how I intended to tell you. But I have to go. I've got to get down there. Now."

He held her gaze for a moment longer, then turned and headed out the door.

Trembling, she followed him onto the side porch, where she gripped a support post and watched him jog to his SUV. Throw his duffel into the passenger seat. Jerk the door closed. The engine roared to life, then he took off, dust and gravel kicking up behind.

Legs barely holding her up, she leaned into the post, her hands wrapping more tightly around it.

Rob had a child.

Why hadn't he told her?

Rob stared down at his sleeping daughter. So tiny in the metal-sided bed, tubes and monitors hooked up to her dainty frame. Her leg remained red and swollen where the bee had stung her ankle, but the doctor said she was doing well. That there were no signs of infection thus far. They'd keep her overnight as a precaution because she was so small.

He'd sent his mom home late afternoon, but he didn't anticipate he'd sleep much tonight in the chair provided for him. He'd already prayed himself out, the rush of adrenaline that accompanied every mile of his trip having gradually subsided once assured of Angie's safety.

But he couldn't shake the look of shocked confusion in Olivia's eyes when he'd told her. Not at all the way he'd planned to share such news. He'd intended to take her on a picnic lunch, down by the creek. Show her pictures of Angie. Gauge her reaction. Answer as honestly as he could any questions—or accusations—she might have.

Even under the best of circumstances, telling her risked rejection. All but guaranteed it, in fact. He could now admit to himself that in his prayers, in his daydreams of recent weeks, he'd tried to believe God would work a miracle. That she'd accept him for who he was, failures and all. And accept Angie, too.

But by the look on her face as it drained of color, that wasn't to be the case. He'd heard it in her trembling voice. Seen it in her wide, troubled eyes. She wouldn't welcome a call from him tonight. He'd tumbled from the pedestal she'd placed him on so many years ago. Shattered into a thousand irreparable fragments.

From where she sat on the footbridge overlooking the creek, jeans-clad legs dangling over the edge, Olivia gazed at the twilight-lit landscape. One hand on Elmo snuggled up beside her, warming her leg on this coolish evening, she could see through a break in the trees the once-sharp edges of clouds now blended into a soft, inky haze. The whir of a hummingbird passed by in the fading light, catching the pup's attention. Then silence. A handful of stars glittered in the eastern sector of the sky. And still she waited…

"Don't You have anything You want to say to me, Lord?" A faint breeze stirred, drying the last of her tears.

Rob has a daughter.

Why hadn't he told her? And why hadn't he married the mother of his child? What kind of choice was that? Her mind flashed to the day at Kit's when she'd commended the young couple for "doing the right thing." What was it he'd said? Something about it only being the right thing if Aiden and Sally weren't lousy parents? What did that mean?

She stroked Elmo's soft coat as her mind flew to the faceless, nameless woman with whom Rob shared a child. What was it about her that enticed him to compromise his once rock-solid beliefs? Lure him over the brink? No. She shook her head, as if to fling that unfair judgment aside. No, it wasn't right to paint this unknown woman as someone skilled at ensnaring men against their will. Rob was a grown man. He'd made a choice.

But why? And why hadn't he chosen to marry her?

Listening to the music of the creek as rivulets danced around the worn-smooth stones—the sound that inspired Singing Rock's name—she replayed in her mind every word he'd said after his mother's call.

It had been all she could do to keep her mind on her responsibilities throughout the day. Dealing with guests. Going through the motions on autopilot as she'd prayed for the child. For Rob. Would he call? Let her know his daughter was okay?

"Hey, pooch." Elmo's ears perked up. "Does a kiss earn the right to barge into his life? Ask questions? Demand answers?"

The pup thrust a wet nose into her hand. Wagged his tail. Pressed more closely against her. She continued to stroke him as she drank in the scent of the creek. Moist foliage. Decaying vegetation. Then she stared again into the infinite heavens, at the stars flung out across the darkening canopy.

"What happened, God? And please don't tell me he's another guy who needs prayer and You knew You could count on me to provide it. Couldn't You have found someone else to do it this time? Why's it always have to be me?"

Her cell phone rang and she made a grab for it without looking at caller I.D. Almost as if expecting God to speed dial her with His answers.

"Hello?"

"Hi, Olivia."

Her heart sank. Paulette. *Please, God, don't let us fight about anything. I can't handle it tonight.*

"Have you seen Rob? He's not answering my calls."

"He's out of town." She didn't intend to tell her sister more than that. She had to assume she wasn't the only one in Canyon Springs Rob hadn't told about his daughter. "Is there something I can help you with? I'm filling in for him."

"I need to check on cabin availability the second weekend of October. Vern's parents are coming from Yuma and, to be quite honest, I can't deal with guests right now."

"I'm sure there's a cabin free. You know how demand drops off after Labor Day." Surely Rob wouldn't deny her sister a complimentary few nights' stay for her in-laws if the place wasn't booked. "I'll check tomorrow and let you know."

"Great. They'll be coming on Friday and leaving Monday."

"I'll take care of it." *Get off the line, Paulette. Rob may be trying to call.*

"Brandi was whining tonight because she hasn't heard from you. But thanks for backing off."

Guilt pierced. Not seeing Brandi hadn't been intentional. Caught up in Singing Rock responsibilities and her own life's drama, she had forgotten to call her. Some aunt she was.

"I'd like to spend time with her. Take her shopping or something, if that's okay."

"We'll see." Paulette's tone brooked no argument. "Don't forget the reservation."

Please, Lord, don't let my sister smother the life out of Brandi as she's tried to do to me.

Olivia stuffed the phone into her jacket pocket, remembering how that morning she'd dressed to impress Rob. How her eyes had sparkled back at her in the mirror in anticipation of seeing him again. How she believed, if only for a few hours, that God had opened the door to a long-awaited dream.

Rob had kissed her.

But knowing what she knew now, what did that mean to him? What had he intended it to mean to her?

He had a daughter he'd told her nothing about. Had kept her a secret for weeks. And what was his relationship with the child's mother? Could marriage still be on the horizon?

If he brought mother and child to Canyon Springs, no way would she stay here, not even as much as she wanted to prove to her parents she wasn't the irresponsible creature Paulette believed her to be. She wouldn't hang around to watch Rob and his little family build a happy home at Singing Rock.

But why hadn't he told her?

Over and over she'd asked herself that question and could come to only two conclusions. She didn't know Rob McGuire like she thought she had. And he didn't trust her.

Chapter Fourteen

When he pulled up outside the lodge, he hadn't expected a welcoming committee. But four days after his emergency run to the Valley, when he drove into the clearing mid-afternoon, the door opened and a handful of chatting women filed out onto the porch. As he parked off to the office side of the building, under the shade of a ponderosa, he spied Olivia among them, looking even more vibrant and beautiful than he'd remembered. Certainly more so than when he'd left her standing there only days ago in bewildered confusion.

A glance into the backseat of his vehicle confirmed Angie was still asleep in her car seat. He rolled down the windows to admit the fresh mountain air, then got out, his ears picking up the female voices ringing clearly from the porch.

"Thanks for lunch and the tour." A slim blonde with blunt-cut hair motioned to her surroundings.

"I've lived in Canyon Springs for years and have never been here. The lodge is perfect for our meetings while we await the remodel."

"You can see, can't you," a redhead with lacquered fingernails pointed out, "why I'm intending to talk my husband into renting a cabin when his side of the family descends for the holidays."

"Don't forget, the lodge is suitable for a variety of special events." Olivia cut a mischievous look at the first speaker. "Like a wedding reception, Sandi?"

The blonde blushed and momentarily covered her face with her hands.

"And I see an added attraction." With a laugh, the red-head nodded toward him as he approached. "Holding out on us, are you, Olivia?"

Not surprisingly, her smiled faltered.

"Good afternoon, ladies."

Olivia self-consciously motioned toward the blonde. "Rob, I'd like you to meet Sandi Bradshaw soon-to-be-Harding. President of the historical society."

She must be the fiancée of the firefighter guy his brother-in-law wanted him to join for a men's Bible study.

"And Cate Landreth. Becky, Fay and Wanda. All members of the Canyon Springs Historical Society. And everyone, this is Rob McGuire, Singing Rock's—new manager."

Would she ever be able to say it without stumbling? The redhead—Cate? He'd heard of her—flashed a troubled look at Olivia. "I thought you'd finally come home to manage the place. Your folks hired someone outside the family?"

He shot a look in Olivia's direction, but she avoided his gaze. She'd come back to manage Singing Rock?

Cate turned to give him a curious but appreciative once-over, then her eyes glinted with awareness. "Oh, oh, I get it now. This good-lookin' guy is soon to be a part of the family?"

Her laugh rang out and Olivia's less-than-happy gaze met his. What could he expect? He wasn't exactly a prize these days and she knew it. From what he'd heard from his sister, though, the Landreth woman was the bane of Canyon Springs single adults. Poking. Prying. She rivaled the online sites for attempted set-ups. He'd steer clear—but after he rescued Olivia.

He placed a foot on the bottom step of the porch. "Now, Cate, don't you go scaring Olivia off like that. When a man has a plan, he doesn't need the local matchmaker jumping the gun and spilling his strategies."

"Sorry, Mr. McGuire." Smirking, she turned to Olivia. "Pretend you didn't hear a word of this, honey."

The ladies laughed, said goodbyes and headed to their cars. As they drove off, he turned to Olivia, not certain what his reception would be. "Cate's quite the character, isn't she?"

"To say the least. And you gave her enough ammunition to keep the town gossiping for weeks."

He doubted it. Once Angie's presence became common knowledge, all else would be forgotten.

"So the historical society met here today? I didn't see that on the calendar when I checked it a few days ago."

"It was a last-minute thing. I didn't think you'd mind," she added quickly. "I invited them here for a tour. Sandwiches."

"Kind of a promo event?"

"The society is in contact with a lot of visitors to our community. Their word of mouth recommendation for lodging could send business our way. That's okay, isn't it?"

"Yeah, sure." He kicked his booted toe at the step, then leveled his gaze on hers, aware that they were both sidestepping the elephant in the room. Or rather, his daughter in the SUV. "Care to elaborate on what Cate said? About you coming home to manage Singing Rock?"

Her eyes widened slightly, his question apparently catching her off guard, but she recovered quickly. "That's what I thought my parents expected of me. But with them hiring you..."

He frowned. "But if I hadn't been here when you returned?"

She didn't answer.

"This explains a lot." Like why she challenged his decisions. Argued with him about the direction Singing Rock should go. "Paulette led me to believe you had no intention of staying for long."

"And she's right. I won't be."

"Because I'm the manager of Singing Rock?"

"Because I have better things to do." She turned toward the lodge door, then hesitated, looked back with questioning eyes. He knew what was coming. Braced himself.

"How is…your daughter?"

Olivia stood off to the side, watching as Rob expertly extracted his pride and joy from the car seat. Shoulder-length, dark brown curls. Red-and-white sundress. Tiny sandals. A gauze-wrapped ankle— where the bee had stung her? What a doll. Gray-eyed like her father, expression alert, inquisitive, but her face rounded with toddler softness.

Snuggled in her daddy's arms, she solemnly studied the woman she didn't recognize, then looked up at Rob, eyes questioning. He focused on Olivia, his own gaze uncertain. Wary. As if unsure of the reception his daughter would receive.

"This is Olivia."

Angie smiled shyly. "Libbia."

"She looks like you, Rob," Olivia said softly, her heart going out to the little one.

"You think?"

"Oh, yeah. Same eyes. Smile." She wished he

wouldn't look so uneasy. So uncomfortable. Then again, it was in many ways an awkward moment for both of them. Presenting his out-of-wedlock child to a woman who'd known him in college as a man who championed the sanctity of marriage. A woman he'd thoroughly kissed but a handful of days ago.

"Mom and Dad pushed for a DNA test until the first time they saw her. Never mentioned the subject again."

Why would his folks push for that? Had there been some question that Angie might not be his?

"Hi, Angie." She gave a small wave and the child giggled, buried her face in Rob's shirt. Then peeked at her.

"You are such a beautiful little girl."

"Can you say thank you?" Rob prompted.

"Tank you."

"You're welcome. What did you do to yourself here?" She pointed at the gauze-wrapped ankle.

Angie lifted her leg and inspected it. "A big bee stinged me."

"Oh, my. Did that hurt?"

The little girl nodded.

"The doctor says the reaction wasn't life-threatening." He shifted Angie in his arms. "That this might be a one-time thing. The allergist thinks it was a more severe reaction since she's so small. But I'll keep a close eye on her. Already stopped by a

Canyon Springs doc this afternoon to fill out paper-work and get her a follow-up appointment."

Olivia patted Angie's foot. "You are a brave girl."

"Yes." Angie gave a jerky nod of confirmation. "Jesus made me better. And Daddy gave me a puppy."

Rob smiled and kissed his daughter's cheek. "A stuffed one."

"May I hold her?"

Olivia sensed his hesitation. A flash of anxiety. "She's kind of a daddy's girl. So don't take it personally if she doesn't go for it. Let's see if you can get her to come to you on her own. Sometimes that works best."

He gently set the child on the ground. Helped her get her balance as he held her hand. Straightened her tiny skirt. "I'll have to dress her more warmly for living up here. It was almost a hundred in the Valley when we left."

If she was to live here, he must at least have joint custody. Or would Angie's mother be joining him, too? She crouched a short distance away from the father-daughter duo. Smiled. Tilted her head. Whispered a few reassuring words to the child who fixed curious eyes on her.

"How old are you, Angie?"

Still gripping her father's hand, she thrust out three fingers. Rob bent to curl one under, making two.

"You're two now but you'll be three someday, won't you?" Olivia nodded emphatically. "Yes, you will."

The tiny girl giggled.

Olivia held out her arms. "Do you want me to hold you, Angie?"

The child studied her—that solemn look so like Rob's—then she looked up at her daddy. He nodded his okay. Then releasing his hand, she headed straight for Olivia, who swept her into a hug.

A relieved-sounding laugh escaped Rob's lips. "Wow. Never seen that before. You must be a kid-whisperer."

Olivia gathered the sweet-scented Angie closer, looking up to see Rob still watching with somewhat anxious eyes. "She's a sweetheart."

"You can see why it killed me to leave her in Phoenix the past several weeks. But I didn't have anyone to take care of her while I worked."

"And you do now?"

"Meg has a friend who can most of the time."

"And I'll take care of her the rest of it." She gave Angie a delighted squeeze. But when Rob's gaze met hers, a too-familiar puckering of his brow telegraphed what he thought of that idea. She should have known better than to make the premature suggestion. She'd been so enraptured by Angie, she'd gotten ahead of herself. He owed her answers and he knew it.

"Thanks for offering, but it will work out. I talked to Mrs. Mabank, and she says she'll cover if I'm called out at night."

He squatted and tugged on the sash of Angie's sundress to get her attention. "Come on, little lady. I promised your aunt Meg we'd stop by her house after I picked up a few things at the office."

"No." Playing with Olivia's necklace, Angie shook her head.

Olivia glanced at Rob, amused at the befuddled look on his face. "That's her favorite word now I suppose—no?"

"It's getting to be."

He pried tiny fingers away from the jewelry. "Come on now, Angie. Don't make Daddy a liar. I've been telling everyone what a good girl you are."

Angie continued shaking her head, but allowed her father to draw her into his arms. He stood and Olivia did, as well. She patted the little girl's sandaled foot. So tiny.

"Will you come visit me again?" The question was as much for her father as for the toddler. Rob was clearly distancing himself. Clearly uncomfortable in her presence. And why shouldn't he be? He was no more the man she'd believed him to be than she was still the wild child of her teenage years. "Your daddy and I need to talk."

Angie nodded emphatically as Rob's somber gaze locked on Olivia's. "Tell Olivia bye-bye, Anj."

"Bye-bye, Libbia."

Had he no intention of arranging time to explain himself? Did he not think he owed her that much? It looked as if this was God's confirmation that it was over between them before it had even begun.

"I wish I'd have had more time." Rob watched as his sister cradled a sleepy-eyed Angie on her lap, Meg's dark tousled hair brushing his daughter's head. "More time to get to know Olivia—for her to get to know me—before I dropped the ultimate bombshell on her."

Meg's troubled expression conveyed her concern. "She didn't take it well?"

He pushed back from the kitchen table, listening to warm laughter echoing from the living room. His brother-in-law, Joe, and nephew Davy had excused themselves after dinner to play video games. Meg had agreed to keep Angie for a few nights so he could baby-proof his apartment. Get her room set up. Secure a safety gate at the top of the stairs. He'd barely had Angie in town more than a few hours and was already relying on his sister, taking advantage of her good nature.

"She intercepted mom's call about Angie's hospitalization. Then she started asking all sorts of questions while I was trying to get out the door. I blurted it out and took off."

"Have you talked to her? Seen her since?"

"Today." He reached over and ran a finger over Angie's soft cheek. The little girl smiled, her eyes now closed. "Right before I came over here."

"How was she?"

"Nice to Angie. But it was awkward. I can tell I really hurt her. Not just by not telling her, but the whole thing. My messing up. Letting her down."

"You care for her a lot, don't you?"

He sat back in his chair, his eyes still on Angie. Watching her gentle breathing. "Didn't intend to. Tried not to. But Olivia's...special."

"Does she know that?"

Face warming at the memory of the kisses they'd shared, he darted a look at his too-observant sister. A knowing smile tugged at her lips. "I think I made myself clear enough—the night before Angie's hospitalization. But I don't think that much matters now. I think finding out about me the way she did erases whatever understanding we'd come to. Can't say I blame her."

"Have you had an opportunity to explain what happened?"

With a fingertip he scrolled an invisible design on the table's surface. "Not yet. She said we need to talk, but I'm not sure she wants to hear what I have to say so much as she wants me to hear what she has to say."

"You need to let her do that."

He grimaced. "To be quite honest, Meg, I don't need another woman telling me I'm not the man for her. Been through that twice, don't care to hear it a third time."

"You can't be sure there will be a third time."

"You didn't see her face when I told her I had a daughter."

"But you said she was nice to Angie."

"Yeah. Talked to her. Hugged her. Said she'd be happy to fill in as a babysitter if I need her to."

"I don't know, Rob..." Meg gave him an encouraging smile. "That doesn't sound like a woman who's rejecting your child. Or who's slamming the door on you, either."

"Yeah, well, it doesn't much matter at this point." He leaned his forearms on the table edge. "I can't risk Angie getting attached to her, then Olivia hitting the door. Makes me understand the protectiveness of single moms I've known through the years. How they wanted to make one-hundred-percent sure a relationship would pan out before they'd introduce their kids to a boyfriend."

"You're saying you think she's too much like Cassie? Capricious? A fly-by-night?"

"Not to that extreme. She's a strong believer in God, whereas Cassie wasn't there yet. But from what I pick up from her oldest sister, she has a history of drive-by relationships. Part-time jobs. I know she switched her college major half a dozen times. Incapable of settling down for more than a few moments before she's off to the next big adventure. She's planning a trip to the Holy Land as we speak."

"So you're thinking it's better to let whatever you'd started die a natural death."

He met Meg's steady gaze head-on. "What is it about me that I can't seem to attract—or be attracted to—women who can commit to me?"

"You know, Rob, I've learned that in life—and love—you sometimes have to take risks." Meg adjusted Angie in her arms. "You may not realize it, but if you write off Olivia, you're setting yourself up for a pattern of allowing fear of rejection to limit you to superficial relationships. You two need to spend time together. Talk. She needs to get to know Angie. And you."

"Nice in theory, but like I told you and our folks a few weeks ago, I have more serious things to be thinking about than a love life. Every time someone Cassie's parents' age appears in the door of the office or I glimpse a New York license plate in town, my heart rate ramps up into the danger zone."

"From what you've told me about their relationship with Cassie, they may easily come to the conclusion that a grandchild isn't worth the time and trouble."

"Maybe. But it's one more reason, until that's resolved, not to involve anyone in my life. I can't have her parents portraying me in court as a footloose and fancy-free bachelor out for a little action."

"Anyone who knows you would know that was a lie."

He closed his eyes momentarily, wishing for the billionth time that he'd never met the captivating Cassie. Had exhibited more self-control. Had been faithful to his beliefs. Then again, what would life be without his sweet little Angela?

"But the truth is, Meg, your big brother got a woman he wasn't married to pregnant. The track record is there for the world to see. For a lawyer to twist and exploit to Cassie's folks' advantage."

"Cassie's track record isn't exactly stellar, either. Abandoning her child."

"Angie's too young to understand what went on when her mother walked out on her. But she'll soon be asking questions I don't yet know how I'll answer. I sure don't want her dealing with the added confusion and grief of a mother substitute who deserts her, too."

His wrong choices had already set his little girl up for a lifetime of mountains to climb.

Meg's thoughtful gaze pinned him. "Are you more concerned with protecting Angie's heart—or your own?"

"Angie's, of course." Rob's jaw tightened and he shot an uncompromising glare at his sister. "Mine's already turned to stone."

Chapter Fifteen

❧

"I can't help but think he didn't tell me because he doesn't trust me, Reyna." Olivia's hand gripped her cell phone, her voice low as she rocked in the front porch swing the next evening.

"Seems he's the one who can't be trusted—keeping the existence of a child that's so much a part of his life from someone he's become interested in."

"I'm not sure he was ever interested."

"You said he kissed you, didn't you?"

Olivia mentally slammed the door on that memory. She couldn't let herself keep returning to it. Dwelling on it. "Yeah, but he did a lot more than kiss Angie's mother and apparently that didn't mean anything. He didn't even marry her."

What kind of man wouldn't marry the mother of his child?

"Have you asked him why he didn't? Maybe she died in childbirth. Something tragic."

"If that were the case, he'd have said so, wouldn't he? Why keep it a secret? So where's the kid's mom?"

"You need to talk to him, Olivia," Reyna said for the umpteenth time since Olivia had called her. "Find out what happened."

"I already told you. He's not making it easy to find time alone with him. Wasn't around much today at all. And when he *was* around—well, this isn't something you discuss in front of friends, family or Singing Rock guests. He's kept himself well-insulated by staying in the thick of things since he returned. I'm not sure he has any intention of ever talking to me."

"Be patient. If he's still the man you believed him to be, this has to be a difficult time for him. The existence of an out-of-wedlock child can't be an easy thing for him to admit to someone he knew when he was a college church group leader."

Olivia sighed. "That's just it. I'm not sure he *is* the man I believed him to be. I'm coming to recognize that I'm not the world's best judge of character." The image of Kendal Paige rose up in her mind. "I'm hurt that he didn't confide in me. Didn't think enough of our relationship to let me know he had a child. That tells me he didn't—doesn't—trust me. You should have seen his face the whole time I was meeting his daughter yesterday. As if expecting me to do something that might hurt her."

"You never know, Olivia, that may have happened to him in the past. Someone else's reaction."

"Which tells me he doesn't know me. I'd never do anything like that."

"No, but that doesn't mean he can't come to know you. And you, him."

"But is all this hassle and hurt worth it? It seems that if a relationship is really a God thing, it wouldn't be this hard."

Reyna laughed. "Oh, my. Don't let your pastor brother-in-law hear you say that. It's one of my hubby's pet peeves when counseling couples—that they think relationships should be effortless. They sometimes act so surprised when they discover they have to work at it."

She hadn't told Reyna, but she wasn't certain she wanted to stay at Singing Rock at all. It no longer mattered whether or not she proved herself to Paulette and her parents. She only wanted out of here. As far away from Rob as she could get.

"I'm willing to work when I'm sure it's the real thing." Her tone sounded defensive even to her own ears. "Right now I'm doubting that what I thought was God's leading to come back here was truly His leading, that's all."

"I don't know the answer to that. But time will tell. Trust me. And God."

When her sister hung up, Olivia sat staring at the lighted apartment window across the way. How could things have gone so wrong? All week she'd prayed. Cried. Prayed some more. Had herself almost convinced that when Rob returned he'd sweep her into his arms, explain everything—that it was all a terrible misunderstanding—and somehow everything would be okay.

But it wasn't okay. Didn't appear it would ever be.

The sound of an approaching vehicle drew her attention. A familiar minivan pulled up in front of the lodge, the faint, accompanying odor of car exhaust catching her attention. She sat up straighter on the porch swing. Paulette?

After several minutes, the driver's-side door opened and in the illumination from the lodge's porch light, she recognized her oldest sister getting out. She paused to speak to another person in the vehicle, then closed the van's door quietly. Moved to the passenger side. Waited. Then reached for the door handle and opened it. Someone exited. Slammed the door.

Brandi?

Paulette motioned to her daughter, who preceded her up the stairs to the lodge. The shoulders of Olivia's niece slumped, the bounce in her step gone. Paulette opened the glass-mullioned door and they disappeared inside.

What were they doing here tonight, with Brandi looking like someone headed for the hangman's noose?

Apprehension prickling, Olivia trotted across the clearing to quietly pull open the lodge door. She stepped inside and spied Paulette, arms folded, mouth set in a grim line. She shot Olivia a sharp look, then focused on Brandi, who stood at the bottom of the steps, watching as Rob descended from his apartment.

His gaze swept the three of them, brows raised in question. "What can I do for you ladies?"

"Brandi has something she wants to say to you." Paulette nodded toward her daughter and Rob turned to the young girl.

A tear trickled down her cheek. "I'm sorry, Rob."

He glanced at Olivia as if for a clue as to what was going on, appearing as perplexed as she felt. "For—?"

Lips trembling, Brandi hung her head. "For trashing Singing Rock's cabins."

He hadn't seen that one coming.

With a troubled glance at Brandi's mother, then Olivia, he motioned to one of the seating areas of the rearranged room. "I think we should all sit down."

Brandi and Paulette followed him, seated themselves on the sofa—miles apart. He eased into an upholstered chair, but Olivia hung back.

The teenager clasped her hands between her knees, looking more like a wide-eyed little kid than the ever-smiling, confident young woman he'd encountered several times since coming to town. She was responsible for a month of headaches and repair work?

"Thank you for telling me, Brandi." His voice broke through the echoing stillness of the room. "The ongoing damage has been a concern for me. I'm glad it's come to an end."

"I'm sorry." Staring down at her lap, she wiped at her eyes.

Man, he hated to see her cry. But he couldn't go all soft just yet. He needed to get to the bottom of this. "Had I done something to upset you? To make you feel you needed to vandalize the property once I became the manager?"

She jerked her head up, shaking it in denial. "No. It had nothing to do with you."

"Tell him why you did it," Paulette prompted, looking for all the world like a sullen, puffed up old owl.

Brandi shrugged. Looked back down at her hands.

Olivia caught his eye, shook her head and moved in closer. Apparently she didn't know what was going on any more than he did.

"She got in with the wrong crowd." Paulette shifted impatiently on the sofa, not taking her incensed eyes off her daughter. "Summer kids."

He glanced again at Olivia, realization dawning. "Those kids who took exception to thinning overgrown acres along the highway?"

Brandi stared at him, eyes pleading. "I tried to stop them."

Paulette scoffed. "How is joining in on damaging your grandparents' property trying to stop them? Almost killing Brett's dog?"

The teen drew back, her eyes begging him for understanding. "I thought it was a fox or coyote. Why would Elmo be out in the middle of the night? I had no idea we might have hit him until Olivia said the vet thought someone did."

"Joy riding and vandalizing. When your father gets back—"

Rob held up a restraining hand, cutting off Paulette's verbal barrage. Then he focused on the girl. "Brandi, why don't you tell me in your own words what happened. Why you participated in tearing up Singing Rock."

Her chin trembled. "Because I wanted Grandma and Grandpa to come home. If there was trouble, I thought they would. They're the only ones in the whole wide world who understand me. Who care."

He sensed Olivia flinch.

"That's not the real reason," Paulette cut in again, her tone shaming. "Stop making excuses and tell them about the boy."

With a teary gaze, Brandi looked at Olivia for the first time. "I'd never had a boyfriend before, Aunt Olivia. Not until this summer. I was afraid if I didn't help him and his friends—"

"That he'd dump you," Olivia supplied, moving to crouch at the feet of her niece. Take her hand.

Brandi gave a jerky nod, her gaze locked on that

of her aunt. Another tear trickled. "He dumped me, anyway. Called me tonight from Phoenix and... dumped me."

"Oh, honey." Ignoring Paulette's disapproving glare, Olivia gathered the now-sobbing girl into her arms. Thank goodness Olivia was here. He wouldn't have known what to do.

A scowling Paulette bobbed her head judgmentally and turned to him. "That's how I found out about all this. That she'd been sneaking out at night. Running with that summer crowd. Her baby sister told me she was crying after she'd been on the phone. I went to find out what was going on and all this came tumbling out. Heaven help me and her father if she did any other 'favors' for that boy besides wrecking Singing Rock."

A red-eyed Brandi jerked from Olivia's arms, obviously offended at the implication. "I didn't. I didn't, Mom. I promise."

Rob's steady gaze held Olivia's for a flashing second. He stood and reached out to take Brandi's hand, helped her to her feet before Paulette could further embarrass her daughter. "Thank you for coming here tonight to tell me the truth."

"Are you going to call the police?" She shot a look at her mom. Had Paulette convinced her he would?

He smiled. "No."

Her own smile wobbled. "I'll work here after school for free. I'll get a job. I'll pay you back. I promise."

"How about we discuss that later? I'm sure you want to get on home, try to get a good night's sleep."

"Thank you." She cut a doubtful look at her mother, granted him a grateful half smile, then fled out the door and into the night.

"I don't know what to say, Rob." Paulette rose to her feet, eyes weary and mouth downturned. "As a parent you try to instill in your kids right and wrong. She may think after this apology that it's all over, that she's off the hook, but—"

"Go easy on her, Paulette," he said softly, his heart going out to Olivia's niece. "I understand there are consequences for her wrong decisions. That you and your husband need to establish parameters for her to regain your trust. But don't let her feel you're rejecting her for what she's done. Don't make her pay for this mistake the rest of her life."

Was that how Rob felt? That he was having to pay for his "mistake" for the rest of his life? To Olivia's surprise, Paulette didn't argue with him as she may have if it had been her baby sister uttering those same words on Brandi's behalf. Instead, she nodded, glanced thoughtfully at Olivia, then followed her daughter outside.

At the sound of the van starting up, Rob moved to the door and quietly shut it. Then turned to her, shaking his head. "Never would have guessed Brandi."

"Me, neither. I feel so awful." She sank down onto the sofa, weak-kneed. "So guilty."

"Why? You didn't have anything to do with this."

"I knew she and her mother were on the outs. She even told me how much she missed her grandparents, wished they'd come back. If only I'd paid more attention. Spent time with her. Hadn't been so caught up in my own world."

"You can't blame yourself. I imagine this has been in the making for quite a while."

"I still remember how it feels to be her age. How confusing everything is. I could have helped." She clutched one of the throw pillows to her chest. "Paulette means well, but she doesn't understand a personality like Brandi's. Instead of nurturing and guiding, she tries to control it. I should have stepped in and run interference between the two. Maybe Paulette's right. I don't have the sense of a goose."

Frowning, he eased down onto the sofa beside her. "Hold on here. I don't see any evidence of that."

"I can give you a few examples if you'd like." She gave a halfhearted laugh. He may as well judge for himself. "For instance, the married guy I was dating right before I came back here. How about that?"

He squinted one eye. "You dated a married guy?"

"Steadily for over a month. I should have guessed something was up when he didn't want the rest of the team to know we were seeing each other."

"The guy lied to you."

She tossed the pillow aside. "Yes, but I was too naive. Should have seen the signs. Questioned more. I felt like such a fool when I found out."

"And deeply hurt."

"That, too."

To her surprise, he reached for her hand, his eyes troubled. "I shouldn't have lied to you, either, Olivia. I was wrong to keep Angie a secret."

Her breath caught as he cradled her hand gently in his big warm one. She met his gaze uncertainly. "I wish you *had* told me. Felt you could trust me."

"It had nothing to do with not trusting you. From the moment you showed up at Singing Rock, I kept telling myself I was putting it off because I didn't want to hurt you. That I didn't want to disappoint you." He gazed down at their clasped hands. "But I know now it was about my pride. I was mortified when I learned I'd fathered a child outside of marriage. Humiliated to my very foundation. Ashamed. I finally realized I'd been indulging in pride my entire adult life. Congratulating myself that I was above temptation. That's not an easy thing to admit. Especially to you."

"There was something you expected of yourself—"

"And discovered it didn't exist. I'd convinced everyone—and myself—that I could never stumble. Fall. But it was a life of counterfeit humility. I'm nothing but a big phony."

She tightened her grip on his hand. "You aren't a phony, Rob."

"The facts dispute that, don't you think? I'd even considered quitting when your folks got back, not bringing Angie here at all. Then you'd never have to know. I was afraid you'd never be able to understand or respect me if you found out."

"I still respect you." She nibbled at her lower lip. "But I have to admit, I don't understand."

"If it wasn't for the reality of Angie, I'd be able to convince myself it happened to someone else. That someone else let their relationship with God go untended, had allowed their values and personal commitments to wither on the vine."

"Things like that don't happen overnight."

"No." He released her hand, stood. Paced the floor. "Ironically, at the time I was caught up in climbing the corporate ladder, my spiritual life spiraled steadily downward. I could stand here and make excuses all night. Tout the toll taken by years in a highly stressful work environment. No time for friends who would keep me accountable. No time for God. Believe me, I've thought up some good ones."

Feeling his heartache, she wished he'd cease his pacing. Sit down by her once again where she could reach out to touch him and console him.

"So, Angie's mother—she worked with you?" It was so easy to picture her. Designer business suit and pricey high heels. Manicured nails. Stylishly cut hair.

Sharp, professional, with an eye on the next promotion. Everything Olivia wasn't.

A regretful smile touched his lips. "Cassie—that's her name, Cassie Wells—wasn't one to be tied down to standard employment. Her mother's family was well off—so she lived an unencumbered lifestyle. Worked whenever and wherever it suited her. When I met her, she'd just returned from Peru. Was employed at a sandwich shop across the street from the building where I worked."

"So that's how you started...dating?"

"If you could call it that. Mostly hanging out at her studio apartment late at night when I'd get off work. She was bright. High-spirited. Interested in everything around her. A lot like you in that respect."

She wasn't sure she wanted to be anything like a woman he'd chosen not to marry.

"Despite her restless nature, she exuded calm. A serenity. An acceptance. She wasn't demanding. And she provided everything that my life then lacked. I couldn't believe I was falling for someone who didn't belong in the world I was fighting my way to get into. But I kept telling myself it would work out."

"And then?"

He drew in a deep breath. "And then, about three months after we met, I lost my job."

"The layoffs."

"That's what it was disguised as. Buried under. But the truth of the matter is I'd started questioning the company's business practices. One coworker's in particular. And just my luck, he was promoted into the vice-presidency position I'd been promised, had been working toward—and he showed me the door."

"That must have been a blow."

"Staggering. The rug was jerked out from under me. Everything I'd sacrificed for was wiped out in a moment. I didn't even see it coming." He took a ragged breath, meeting her steady gaze with an uncomfortable one of his own. "And that night, when I got to Cassie's…"

Chapter Sixteen

"One thing led to another," she said softly.

He lowered his gaze, unable to meet her compassion-filled eyes. He didn't deserve her sympathy. Her understanding. He deserved to be shown the door. "And when…when morning came, I realized I'd compromised my deepest core beliefs. Carelessly tossed them away."

"I'm sorry, Rob."

"No more sorry than I am." He again eased down onto the sofa beside her. "When I apologized, tried to explain that would never happen again, Cassie laughed. She thought it was amusing that I had what she called a hyperactive moral code. Thought I was making a big deal out of nothing. The more I tried to make her understand, the more she withdrew. She'd already stuck around longer than originally intended, so the relationship probably would have ended then and there, except that—"

"She was pregnant with your child."

He leaned forward, propping his elbows on his knees and burying his face in his hands. Felt Olivia place a reassuring hand on his back. "As soon as I found out, I asked her to marry me. But she said she didn't want to be a mom...or a wife."

He looked at Olivia, sitting so still beside him as he poured out a story she should never have had to hear. "When she said that, I panicked, scared she'd do something stupid to harm our baby. But she believes there's a God, just hasn't yet bought into the personal Heavenly Father concept. She'd never destroy life. But she made me promise that no matter what happened between the two of us, I'd keep the baby."

"And you promised."

He sat back, his gaze boring into hers. "I can't tell you how hard I prayed that she'd change her mind. Get over her fear of commitment. Fall in love with me. With Angie. But six weeks after our daughter was born, she took off."

"I'm so sorry."

"Me, too." He sucked in a breath. Forced a smile. "So now you know it all, Olivia. The life and times— and downfall—of Robert T. McGuire."

"It wasn't your fault she wouldn't stay."

"I should have found a way to convince her. I can only conclude she saw something lacking in me, just as Gretchen did in college."

"You're wrong. She wouldn't have left Angie with

you if she'd thought that. She felt secure that you'd be a good father."

"But a lousy husband?" He could almost taste the bitterness of that knowledge.

"I'd say there was more going on than met the eye. Stuff from her past. A troubled young woman."

"But I *prayed,* Olivia. Prayed that God would open her heart to me. To Angie. It didn't happen."

This time it was Olivia who reached for his hand. Gripped it tightly with both of hers. "God gave her free will the same as he gives it to you and me. She had an opportunity to have a family and she chose not to accept it." She paused, her uncertain gaze probing. "Are you still praying she'll come back?"

His jaw tightened. Why did God answer some prayers and not others? And yet, could he and Cassie have made it in a one-sided marriage? With his spiritual reawakening, his desire to settle down in one place to raise a family in direct opposition to everything that was Cassie—could it have been possible?

"She won't be back. I've accepted that now." He stared down at their hands, his thumb stroking the soft fingers clasped around his. "I've forgiven her. Although some days it doesn't feel like it."

"Forgiveness is a decision, not a feeling."

"I know."

"But you still need forgiveness yourself, don't you?"

"I know God's forgiven me."

"Maybe in your head, but in your heart?" Her dark eyes studied him. "I just heard you tell Paulette not to make Brandi pay for her mistakes for the rest of her life. But aren't you doing that very same thing to yourself?"

"I'm accountable for my actions. I take full responsibility for what I did. Now I have to live with the consequences."

"You're right. You made a poor choice. Fell short of God's ideal—just like the rest of us." Her grip tightened on his. "But until you can forgive yourself, you'll never be the kind of husband you someday want to be—or the kind of father you want your daughter to have. Can't you see, Rob? How can you expect God to bless your future if you won't turn loose of your past?"

"It's not like I was sixteen years old when this happened. I don't deserve to be let off the hook."

"Deserve? You know better than that. We don't make requests of God based on our own righteousness, but on His mercy."

"I know, but—"

"What if Angie, after deliberately disobeying you, believed she'd disappointed you so much that you couldn't possibly love her anymore? Couldn't forgive her because she didn't deserve it? Pushed you away when you tried to reassure her? How would that make you feel?"

He frowned. "Deeply hurt. I love her."

"So, what you're telling me is you're a better father to Angie than God is a father to you."

He hung his head. Sat in silence. "When you put it that way, it's clearly wrong, isn't it?"

"Very wrong." Her voice remained firm. "God is true to His promises. He's not a liar. Angie's going to need you whole and healed. God still has good plans for you, but only if you let Him bring them about."

"All I can say is I'm sorry, Olivia. I knew I needed to tell you, but you've always thought of me almost like Jesus's little brother who has no faults. Makes no mistakes. Pride kept me from speaking up. I know I'm a big disappointment to you."

"A bigger disappointment to yourself, I think. But you have to let that go."

They sat in shared silence, listening to the antique clock on the mantel tick off the minutes.

Please, Father God, help me to receive the gift of forgiveness Your Son made possible. To stop living in fear of rejection by You and those around me. To be the father to Angie You want me to be. And...

He cleared his throat. "After everything that's happened, I have no right to ask this, Olivia, and I want you to answer honestly."

She nodded.

"Can you forgive me?"

Her grave eyes met his. "I already have."

The tightness in his chest eased. He had God's forgiveness. Now Olivia's. Had his little Angie. Did he have a right to ask God for one more gift? He swallowed back the lump in his throat. "How do you feel about—us? Only days ago…I was so sure—"

"That God had a plan?"

He nodded.

"I think He still has a plan." Olivia's low, hesitant voice soothed his ears. "If we still want it."

Hope sparked, but he couldn't let himself embrace it. Not yet.

"I want it." He lifted her velvet-soft hand to his lips. Pressed a kiss to it. "But what do you want?"

Gazing into her searching eyes, he steeled himself, the residual pain of Gretchen's and Cassie's rejections hammering at the walls he'd built around his heart to keep it out. Hold it at bay.

"What do I want?" Olivia's eyes smiled into his. "What I've always wanted, Robert McGuire. God's grace. And you."

Chapter Seventeen

"Wait for Davy, Angie." Olivia tried her best not to hover over the two-year-old while at the Canyon Springs community park Friday afternoon. But the determined little thing insisted on tagging along to what she called a "big kids'" slide with her older cousin—six-year-old Davy Diaz—and Olivia's niece, five-year-old Mary Kenton. The slippery structure wasn't much higher than Olivia was tall, but just enough to make Olivia nervous as she lifted Angie up to set her on the slide.

"I'm careful, Libbia." The dark-haired child waved and smiled at her. Rob's smile.

"I've got her." Davy settled himself in behind the tot, secured her between his legs, then wrapped his arms around her. With a squeal the twosome set sail, Olivia trotting along beside them. At the bottom, a giggling Angie struggled to free herself from Davy, ready to head back to the slide's steps.

"Again!"

Davy's dark eyes flashed a helpless look in Olivia's direction. She took the hint and caught up with Angie, swept her into her arms. "We need to let Davy rest, okay?"

He and Mary had been such sports, hanging out in the toddler equipment area on their afternoon off for the Canyon Springs homecoming parade rather than the older children's with its more challenging slides and faster merry-go-rounds.

Chubby legs kicked the air in protest. "Again!"

Easing Angie to the ground, but keeping a firm hold on her, Olivia pointed to the sun-shaded blanket where the child's aunt Meg relaxed with Olivia's sister Reyna and her youngest, three-year-old Missy.

Olivia laughed to herself. It wouldn't be hard to imagine this was some kind of a test. That Rob had left his daughter with her for a few days merely to see how she'd cope with the active youngster. A test complete with Rob's sister "accidentally" stopping by the park to keep an eye on how she was doing.

Angie, her face a thundercloud, shoved against Olivia's legs, endeavoring to get around her. "Again!"

Olivia shifted, blocking the way to the slide while Davy made his escape.

"Looky, Angie! Look what Missy has." Thank goodness Reyna understood the ways of a two-year-old, having been through it twice. As Olivia was quickly learning, distraction seemed to be key.

The child paused to check out what Missy was up to. Reyna picked up one of the colorful, doughnut-size plastic rings and wiggled it to get Angie's attention.

Olivia held her breath as Angie trotted away to join the others on the blanket. Whew. Even though she'd often helped take care of other people's children on mission trips, it never ceased to amaze her how much energy a two-year-old had. And how much determination. Obstinacy. Every bit the equal to their adult counterparts.

If things worked out between her and Rob, was she really up to this? No time to adjust to their relationship, work out the kinks of becoming a couple—instead, just a leap into instant motherhood? Not for the first time, she harbored niggling doubts. She loved Rob. Loved Angie. But he came with a bunch of baggage, the least of which was his little girl. Could they make it work or was she still living in a dream world?

Shoving away the nagging thoughts, Olivia joined the toddler who'd situated herself next to Reyna. "Thanks, Rey."

Meg smiled over at Angie. "I can't get over how much she looks like Rob."

"She does, doesn't she?" Olivia constantly marveled at the same thing. If there were telltale signs of resemblance to her absentee mother, she sure couldn't detect them. Olivia didn't like to think about Angie's biological mother. About her relationship with Rob.

But like it or not, Cassie was a reality that had to be dealt with. Would God give her the grace to handle it in a mature and wisdom-filled manner?

Angie patted Olivia's leg to get her attention, then held out a red doughnut. Olivia took it from her, then the child stood, turned her back to Olivia and, putting herself in reverse, plopped into her lap.

"She really likes you, Olivia." Meg smiled knowingly. "Would I be being nosy if I asked how things are between you and Rob?"

"Yes." Heat rose in Olivia's cheeks as she laughed at the intense gazes of both Rob's sister and her own. For the past two weeks she and Rob had been laboring side by side, working up detailed plans for Singing Rock. Sharing meals. Playing with Angie. While no words of love had been uttered by either—and he hadn't so much as tried to kiss her—there seemed to be an understanding between them. So why the underlying uneasiness? The gnawing of waiting for the other shoe to drop?

"We're taking it slow. But—"

"Maybe wedding bells on the horizon?" Meg clapped her hands and a laughing Angie, rocking where she sat, mimicked her.

"Let's not get ahead of ourselves," Olivia warned, apprehension mounting with Meg's assumption. Wedding bells. Rob. That's what she wanted more than anything else in the world, wasn't it? "We may have technically known each other seven years, but…"

Meg sighed. "Rob needs to marry you. And the sooner the better."

"Because—?" She glanced pointedly down at his daughter, brushing her fingers through the toddler's hair. Rob had told her before he left that Cassie's parents might seek legal means to claim her. Was Meg thinking a marriage would ensure that could never happen?

Did Rob think that?

"No, silly." Meg smiled her reassurance. "Although an M-O-M for her would be nice, too. You'd make a fabulous one. But no, I mean you're exactly what my big brother needs. He's gotten to be such a serious stick-in-the-mud. Even stuffy at times. Way too serious for his own good. You're the breath of fresh air he needs in his life."

"I never thought of him as a stick-in-the-mud in college. Reserved, maybe. But he was more easygoing back then. And I'm proud to say that a few days ago he gave two complimentary nights to Singing Rock guests who were delayed in leaving when their car broke down."

"He never would have done that before. Which is exactly why he needs a woman like you in his life." Meg leaned toward Reyna. "Looks like we have our prayers cut out for us. Does a pastor's wife carry any extra clout in the Heavenly realms? See if you can call in a few favors."

Uncomfortable with the continuing line of conversation, Olivia nevertheless managed a laugh, then disentangled herself from Angie. She rose to her feet and picked up the little girl. "Come on, cutie, it's time we get going. We need to get home, get you cleaned up and down for a nice long nap."

Fortunately, Angie didn't protest but cuddled down into Olivia's arms, laid her head on her shoulder. So tiny. So precious.

The three women said their goodbyes and, relieved to escape, Olivia strode across the grassy space to her vehicle. As always, her spirits rose when she glimpsed the Singing Rock logo emblazoned on the side of the SUV. Pride in her parents' accomplishments swelled, renewing her determination to keep their dream for the property afloat. Was that something she and Rob would do together?

As she secured Angie in her car seat in the back, she couldn't help but let her thoughts drift. The sense of peace that descended in the days after she and Rob had talked openly about their pasts had fluctuated. Ebbed and flowed. One moment, delirious with joy. In the next wrought with questions—not about Rob, but about herself. About her ability to be what Rob and Angie most needed in their lives.

She touched fingers to her lips, recalling the sweetness of the last time he'd kissed her. Not merely the physical sensation of it, but the spiritual awareness that it marked a turning point in their relationship. No, neither had said the "L" word. But it hung in the charged air between them. Was their budding love foundation enough on which to build a lifetime commitment? To face the challenges they'd inevitably be confronted by in raising a child who'd been abandoned by her mother?

"Excuse me, please."

Startled, Olivia turned to a smiling woman a few years her senior. A sprinkling of freckles. Sun-streaked blond hair French-braided down her back. A peasant-style blouse topped a broomstick skirt swirling at her ankles.

Olivia returned the friendly smile and the woman motioned to the logo on the door of the vehicle.

"I see that you're a local."

"Yes, I am. Is there something I can help you with?"

"Could you recommend a hotel? Maybe a restaurant that isn't a clone of one you find on every street corner in America?"

"You might try Canyon Springs Inn. Or Kit's Lodge—which also has a top-notch restaurant. And Camilla's Café is a treat. It's on Main Street, across from Dix's Woodland Warehouse."

"Sounds like I have some good options."

"Homecoming crowd this weekend, though, so vacancies may be tight. There's availability at Singing Rock, a cabin resort a few miles outside of town. My folks own it."

"I'll keep that in mind." The woman motioned to Angie. "Your daughter's beautiful."

Olivia's heart warmed at the mistaken identity. This was the second time that day someone had made such an assumption. A lady at the post office earlier. Now this woman.

"She's not mine." She hated to admit it, treasuring the persistent daydream that she and Rob shared the sweet child. "I'm babysitting for my—" Her what? Coworker? Friend? *Boyfriend?* "Just babysitting."

The woman nodded, her gentle gaze lingering on the gray-eyed Angie. Then with a thank-you and a friendly wave, she turned and strolled across the park to her car.

Olivia shrugged, guessing a cabin wasn't her cup of tea, then finished securing Angie. Gazing down at the precious face, her imagination took flight. What did God have in mind for her and Rob? Would in the not-too-distant future she be this dear child's mom? Share other children with Rob?

Please, God, don't let me get my hopes up this time only to have everything fall apart.

"How are you and Angie doing this morning?" Rob squinted against the desert sun piercing through palm tree fronds outside his parents' Phoenix area home. This was the first time since leaving Vegas that he'd left his daughter with someone who wasn't a family member so he wanted to check in. Then again, Olivia was—almost family? His heart ramped up a notch as her oh-so-appealing face flashed into his mind. He recalled her words of understanding… healing…and relived the times his lips had touched hers.

In spite of the anticipation the latter memory renewed, he was determined not to get ahead of himself this round, but to prayerfully seek guidance. He hadn't kissed Olivia since the night he'd confessed the details of his relationship with Cassie. He still struggled on where to set healthy boundaries.

You're in charge, God.

But it felt…inevitable. A peaceful rightness. Not a blind, doggedly determined, I'll-do-whatever-I-want-to kind of right. Rather, a quiet sense of assurance that all was going to work out beyond his wildest hopes and dreams. For the best. His. Angie's. Olivia's.

"We're doing great." Olivia's sparkling tones further lifted his spirits and drew him back to the phone call he'd placed. "Yesterday afternoon we went to the homecoming parade, then to the park for a picnic and playtime where we ran into your sister and mine with their kids. Took a nap after that—both of us. Believe me, I needed it."

He chuckled. "She can be a handful, can't she?"

"To say the least. Then we played until dinnertime. Read stories at bedtime. She didn't sleep real well last night—woke up asking for you—but now we've finished a late breakfast and are ready for our day. If I can sweet-talk Brett into covering for me again, I might take her to see one of my old high school friends whose cat had kittens last week."

"Sorry I'm missing it. Sounds like you're having fun."

"We're having a blast."

A blast with *his* daughter. Guess he shouldn't have been worried about leaving the two alone together. "I can't tell you how much that means to me, Olivia. Your understanding and everything. Forgiving me. Not holding it against Angie."

"I'd never do that, Rob. She's a precious gift from God. Evidence that in spite of our mistakes He can still bring about good things."

How could he have ever thought she was anything like Cassie? Hadn't trusted God when He kept nudging him in Olivia's direction? Why had he lived in fear so long even as he came to know her better?

"You know what?" His words came softly.

"What?" He caught the playful lilt to her tone.

"I'm missing you both right now." His voice sounded embarrassingly husky with emotion even to his own ears. He held his breath lightly, waiting, anticipating the hoped-for response.

"I miss you, too."

Now. Say it now, McGuire. He told Angie he loved

her all the time. Couldn't say it enough. Wanted her to grow up never doubting her daddy adored her. So why couldn't he bring himself to tell Olivia what was filling his heart almost to the point of exploding?

"Rob?"

He swallowed. "Yeah?"

"You'll be home tonight?"

"Mmm-hmm."

"Would you like to join me for dinner?"

Tonight. He'd take her in his arms—and tell her how he felt about her. "That sounds nice. Real nice."

Would she think it dorky if he brought fresh flowers? Dressed up Angie and himself more than usual? Was it too early to openly broach the subject of a shared future? Sure, they'd known each other since college, but she'd only come back into his life six weeks ago. Would she think he was rushing things? He could almost hear his heart beating as the silence stretched across the miles between them. What was she thinking at this very moment? Did anticipation of seeing him this evening well up in her as it did him?

She'd said she missed him, too.

Maybe she really did.

He cleared his throat. "I have more business to take care of down here this morning. A few more things to pick up. Then I'll head back up the mountain."

"Drive carefully."

"Always." No way would he do anything stupid and risk not getting home safely to the ladies in his life. Risk not delivering in person a bouquet of flowers—and his heart—to Olivia Diaz.

Chapter Eighteen

Olivia returned her cell phone to her pocket, picked up Angie and spun the giggling girl around the hardwood floor of Singing Rock's lodge.

"I love your daddy, Angie. Did you know that?" She snuggled her face against the child. "I love him, love him, love him."

Angie patted Olivia's face. "Love him."

"Yes, we do, don't we? We love your daddy."

She loved him. No doubts. No red lights this morning. And she had a sneaking suspicion he might be coming to the same conclusion about her. Her heart danced in time with her steps pirouetting across the polished floor. Was this a dream? Was she imagining the tenderness, the promise in his tone?

Was she setting herself up for the hardest fall of her life?

She drew to a halt. Then shook her head.

No, she wouldn't think about that possibility.

This was a time to trust. To believe. To rejoice. She needed to take one day at a time and stop trying to figure everything out. Rob said he missed Angie—and her. He'd be home tonight. She'd prepare him a feast. Treat him like a king. Show him how much she cared for him and his precious little girl.

Joy bubbled as she once again waltzed his sweet daughter around the room. Moments later she found their jackets and got them bundled up against the cool morning air.

"Let's go grocery shopping. We'll make your daddy a dinner he'll remember forever, okay?"

"'kay."

They'd just stepped out on the broad front porch, hand in hand, as a fiftyish couple exited a flashy, silver convertible. Impeccably dressed in casual sportswear, they looked ready for a day at the country club. Perhaps they were looking for one of the area's gated communities and got lost?

"Good morning! What can I do for you folks?"

The heavyset, salt-and-pepper-haired man glanced at his companion as they approached, then squared his shoulders. "We're looking for Robert McGuire."

"Rob? He's away this morning. I'm Olivia Diaz, Rob's—assistant. Are you looking for lodging? I can help you with that."

"No, no. Personal business with—Rob." The man smiled at Angie. "Who's this cute little lady?"

"Angie."

"Yours?"

"No." Maybe someday. Soon. "Rob's."

The man and woman exchanged glances, then focused on Angie with more than casual interest. A wave of unease coursed through Olivia and she picked up the toddler. Held her close. Were these the people Rob had warned her about? Cassie's parents?

"How do you know Rob?"

The man stuffed his hands in his pockets. "He and our daughter were, shall we say, acquainted."

Icy fingers tiptoed along Olivia's spine. Their daughter. Angie's birth mother.

She tightened her grip on the toddler. Gave the man her most winning smile as she fought the urge to rush back into the lodge and bolt the door. "I'd be happy to tell Rob you stopped by, mister—"

"Wells. Colin Wells. This is my wife, Elaine. And I believe this—" he nodded toward Angie "—is the granddaughter we've come to take home."

"Good doing business with you." Rob secured the U-Haul trailer doors with a chain and padlock. Then turned to offer his hand to the Scottsdale clerk who'd helped him load the last of the supplies he hadn't been able to find locally. He was now all set for those off-season Singing Rock repairs.

Rob climbed into his SUV, then turned the key in the ignition and glanced at the dashboard clock. He'd finished up early. Time to head back up to the high country. Get out of the heat and the bumper-to-bumper traffic descending on the Valley of the Sun with the first wave of Snowbird RVs and travel trailers. But not before he swung by an upscale florist shop and picked out something to catch the eye of a special lady of his acquaintance.

"Olivia Diaz…McGuire." He let the syllables roll off his tongue. Then grinned as he pulled out of the parking lot and onto a busy side street. That combination of names had a nice ring to it, didn't it? "Olivia McGuire."

He switched on the air-conditioning. Then the radio, finding a thumping country band belting out an old tune about saying goodbye to past regrets and coming home at last.

Home. Olivia. How quickly they'd come to be one and the same. He shook his head, marveling at the events of the past few months. How God had not only spared him in Vegas, found him a safe new home in Canyon Springs, but brought the woman of his dreams into his life, as well. Olivia, with her big beautiful brown eyes and forgiving heart.

Olivia Diaz…McGuire.

He grinned again. He was one fortunate man. One who didn't deserve this truckload of blessings—but who was he to argue with God Almighty?

Please, God, help me.

"Rob didn't tell me you were coming, Mr. Wells."

The man placed a foot on the bottom step. Olivia took a step back.

The man chuckled. "I can see we've confused you. Don't mean to. But you see, your friend Rob fathered this little gal with my daughter."

"Cassie?"

His eyes narrowed. "So, you know her name. Know the story. Then you must also know Mr. McGuire didn't have the legal authority to take this child from her mother."

Angie squirmed in her arms, but she didn't set her down.

"She's his daughter. That's authority enough when your mother abandons you."

"Abandon? That's what he told you?" Colin Wells looked sadly at his wife. "Our daughter didn't abandon this sweet child. Your 'friend' took advantage of our daughter. Got her pregnant. Then intimidated her. Threatened her when she wouldn't marry him so he could get hold of a considerable inheritance from her mother. That's when he abducted her child."

"That's a lie."

The man's gaze sharpened at her blunt response. *Oh, good going, Olivia. Make him mad.*

"I wish it was a lie, young lady. Unfortunately, we hadn't been in close contact with our daughter for several years. We only recently learned of the existence of our grandchild. Learned our daughter had been forced to give up her baby. This Rob McGuire wasn't easy to find, but we promised her we'd get her child back."

"Your daughter—" Olivia kept her tone even, not wishing to further provoke them "—abandoned her child and the man who loved her."

"Love?" The man's mouth twisted. "You call it love when a man gets an unmarried woman in a family way, then sneaks off in the night with her child?"

"If that's what she told you, then she hasn't told you the truth."

"What I'm telling you, young lady, is that not only did your Rob abduct this child, but he transported her across state lines. Which makes you—" he raised a bushy brow "—an accessory of sorts if you refuse to relinquish her."

"Rob did not—"

"I know this comes as a shock—Olivia, is it?" The woman's placating tone rang annoyingly. "Especially if you're in a…relationship…with our grandchild's father. It's not our intention to drag the law into this if we can help it, but—"

"Why not?" Olivia shifted Angie in her arms and managed to pull her cell phone from her jacket pocket. She held it up. "I can call 911 right now. Save you the trouble."

The couple shared a fleeting glance, then the woman shook her head. Sighed.

"Look, we're not trying to cause trouble," the

man assured. "We have no intention of snatching our grandbaby from your arms. But we want you to understand the truth of the situation. Obviously your 'friend' has misled you. Like he misled our daughter. Deceived her."

"Rob did not—"

"We thought Mr. McGuire would be here, Olivia," the woman cut in again, her voice now impatient. "You said he's out this morning? When will he return?"

"Soon."

"Then, we'll go into town. Have lunch—and return this afternoon. We understand you're in a difficult position, caring for the child in Mr. McGuire's absence. But rest assured we'll be back. And likely accompanied by law enforcement."

Chapter Nineteen

"Which one do you think spells out most clearly a man's serious intentions?"

The aloof-looking clerk at the Scottsdale florist shop pressed her ruby-colored lips together momentarily. Then raised a brow, her eyes sweeping discreetly over his work clothes. "I assume you're alluding to a proposal?"

A lump formed in his throat at the unanticipated question.

Was he thinking of proposing?

Sure, he intended to tell her he loved her this evening. But the playing with the name thing—he'd only been kicking it around, hadn't he? Trying it on for size. He hadn't bargained on proposing yet. More like easing up on it. One step at a time. Then again, hadn't both his sisters long complained that a man should never tell a woman he loved her unless he intended to put a ring on her finger?

Was he ready for this? Was *she?*

What if Olivia turned him down flat?

His stomach did a rollover. And for a flashing moment, he envisioned the look on the clerk's face if he turned tail and bolted out the door. Serious intentions. That's what he'd told the woman a moment ago. That's what he had for Olivia, wasn't it? Real, serious, God-led intentions.

So what was he waiting for?

The clerk discreetly cleared her throat. Compressed her lips in a tight, disapproving smile. He opened his mouth—but no sound came out.

Do not be afraid, for I am with you.

The assurance that he was on the right track washed through him again. Hadn't his grandpa asked his grandma to marry him on their first date? Look how long they'd been married.

He nodded. "Um, yes, ma'am. A proposal."

Her chilly smile warmed. "Roses. Long-stemmed red roses. A dozen."

His sisters would approve of roses. "Sounds good."

He'd barely settled into his vehicle again—reeling at the sum he'd placed on his credit card and cranking up the AC to keep the boxed flowers at a florist-level chill—when his cell phone rang.

Olivia. He smiled to himself. Had she sensed what he was up to? Was calling to check on him?

"Hey, beautiful. I'm on my way."

"Oh, Rob. Thank God. Hurry. Please hurry."

He sat up straighter at the desperation in her voice. "What's wrong?"

"Cassie's parents—Angie's grandparents. They're here. They've come to take her."

An invisible fist slammed into his chest. *No, God, please, no.* He struggled to regain his breath. Tamp down the panic threatening to paralyze him. *He was close to three hours from Canyon Springs.*

"Don't let them touch her, Olivia."

"I won't. I won't. I have her right here with me."

"Are Cassie's parents there, too? With you?"

"Not right now. But they'll be back. They say they'll bring law enforcement with them. What do I do, Rob, if cops show up? If they try to take Angie before you get here?"

"Sit tight. I'll get hold of Meg and Joe. They'll know who I can contact at the police department. Maybe a local lawyer. Keep Angie with you. Don't let her out of your sight. And don't meet with Cassie's parents alone, you understand?"

"Yes. How far away are you now?"

"Too far. I haven't started home yet."

Her quick intake of breath came clearly across the miles and his grip tightened on the phone. "Everything's going to be okay. I'm on my way."

"Cassie's parents are saying awful things. Saying you threatened her. That you abducted Angie."

His gut twisted. "She left me. Left Angie."

"I know, but that's not what they'll tell the police.

You have to get hold of Cassie, Rob. She's the only one who can straighten this out. The only one the police will believe."

An invisible hand closed around his throat. The only one the police would believe—*or Olivia would believe?*

"She seldom answers my calls. I hear from her when she wants to be heard from."

"There has to be a way to get hold of her." Desperation colored her tones. If only he was there in person. Could hold her. Reassure her. "Maybe you can find her through mutual friends? Place of employment?"

"I never knew her friends. She's not in Vegas anymore. Somewhere in California." A frequently transient soul amidst—what?—forty million?

"We have to find her, Rob."

"I'll do what I can." Which wasn't much. "Where are you now?"

"At Singing Rock. Brett's in the office, so we're not alone."

"Good. I'm on my way."

"Drive carefully, Rob. But please, *please* hurry."

Olivia picked up Angie and headed upstairs to Rob's apartment, a plan formulating. If Cassie wouldn't answer Rob's calls, maybe she'd answer hers? Would pick up when she didn't recognize the name or number?

It took a few minutes to pop Angie in her portable playpen and get her situated. Then Olivia turned to Rob's old wooden desk, her determination growing. But when she reached for the key already snugly inserted in the shallow, middle drawer, she hesitated. She always honored another's privacy. How would he feel if she searched for a phone number?

She glanced at Angie, chatting happily to herself as she stacked plastic blocks. Giggled as they toppled down.

What choice did she have? She couldn't risk Cassie's parents taking Rob's daughter. She *had* to track down Angie's biological mother. And if Rob later objected, so be it.

The open drawer revealed neatly compartmentalized office supplies. Paper clips. Pens. A few stray keys. She pulled the drawer out farther and, with bated breath, glimpsed an accordion file folder, an elastic band stretched securely around it.

Please, Lord, make this easy.

With shaky hands she slipped off the band. Peeped inside. Receipts. Spirits plummeting, she replaced the folder and moved to one of the side drawers. Proceeded to go carefully through each of the three—but came up empty-handed. Through the open window, she heard the sound of gravel crunching under tires. Heard an engine cut off.

Had they returned so soon?

Heart pounding, she dashed to the window. But to

her relief it was a guest unloading a basket outside the laundry facility.

She glanced toward the short hallway that led to Angie's and Rob's rooms. The bathroom. She'd been in Angie's a number of times in recent days. Minimal furnishings. A closet that held extra blankets and toys. Miniature outfits on tiny hangers.

She'd never been in Rob's. Surely he kept personal documents somewhere at the apartment. Despite the advent of computers, this was hardly a paperless society. He owned a car. Would have ownership and insurance papers. Health insurance documents. A birth certificate for Angie.

With another glance at his two-year-old playing happily, Olivia reluctantly found herself standing in the doorway of Rob's room. Light streamed through the wooden, slatted shutters, revealing an almost Spartan arrangement. A double bed, its sheets tucked in military fashion. A precisely folded Navajo blanket at its foot. A single pillow. A nightstand with a lamp, Bible and framed photo of Angie. Small dresser. A chair.

Forgive me, Rob.

She dropped to the floor and peeked under the bed. But unlike hers, which was crammed with overstuffed plastic storage bins, there wasn't so much as a shoebox beneath it. Again on her feet, she unwillingly eyed the dresser. Took a hesitant step toward it, then turned instead toward the accordion-doored closet. Closets were less personal, weren't they? Renewing her determination, she opened the doors wide—and caught the scent of Rob. His aftershave. Leather jacket. The outdoors where he spent so much of his time.

Lined up in front of her were his knit, collared shirts and a few jackets. A couple of pairs of dress slacks draped over pants hangers and jeans were folded and stacked on a top shelf. But it was the back corner of the closet that caught her attention.

Her heart leaped. A steel-gray metal box, one that appeared designed for file folders. She dropped to her knees and tugged on the sturdy handle that topped it. Hardly budged. So it had to be fireproof.

She reached up to flip on the closet light, then found the metal container's latch. That didn't budge, either. Locked.

Now what? This *had* to be what she was looking for.

"Libbia? Please? Libbia?"

"I'm coming."

With a frustrated glare at the metal file, she hurried back to the living room. Angie pointed to a red block that had escaped the confines of the playpen. Olivia picked it up and handed it to the little girl. "Here you go, sweetie."

"Tank you."

Tears pricked her eyes. Rob would be so proud she remembered. "You're welcome."

Gazing at the smiling child, she fought back a helplessness that threatened to render her useless to Rob. The fireproof file had to contain the answers she so desperately needed. Her gaze drifted to Rob's desk—and hope sparked. Those loose keys...

In a flash she took the handful of miscellaneous keys to the bedroom and in no time had the steel box opened. As she'd expected, business documents. Angie's birth certificate—her mother's name Cassandra Jannette Wells. But no phone numbers.

In frustration, her fingers searched the bottom for any scrap of paper that may have escaped its file. Her efforts were rewarded as she withdrew a piece of folded notebook paper.

It opened to an airy, feminine script.

I'm sorry, Rob. I just can't do it. I'm not mom or wife material. You know it as much as I do. Angie's all yours. Remember your promise. Cassie

Olivia sat staring at the page. How could Angie's mother leave such a note? Walk off and abandon the two most important people God had brought into her life? But it was proof. Something to give the police if they showed up with Cassie's parents.

Or would they claim *she* wrote it herself?

With shaky hands, Olivia slipped the note into one of the folders, then sat in numbed silence for a long moment, prayers going up for the troubled young woman. In a final, futile attempt to find contact information, she felt along the sides of the file—and withdrew a five-by-seven color photograph.

A family portrait.

Rob, newborn Angie and an oddly familiar-looking woman who could only be Cassie. Did Angie look more like her mother than she originally suspected? In the stiffly arranged photo, Rob appeared anxious, protective of the bundle in his arms. A beaming Cassie was only weeks from fleeing.

Olivia studied the photo, trying to understand the dissolution of this little family. Somehow she'd thought Cassie would look, well, evil. But the attractive blonde with a smattering of freckles appeared anything but a fiend. Rather, she looked gentle, kindhearted. Full of life. She looked—

Like the woman who'd asked for directions in the park yesterday afternoon.

Olivia stared at the photograph, now grasped between shaking fingers. She couldn't be mistaken. The woman who'd approached her had been Cassie. Was she here to back up her parents' claim to Angie?

Fumbling to relock the steel box, Olivia's mind raced. Regardless of Cassie's intent, she was in Canyon Springs. And Olivia had to find her.

Back in the main room she checked on Angie, then retrieved her cell phone and punched in Rob's speed dial. She had to let him know this latest turn of events. Warn him. But the call went instantly to messaging. He was probably talking to Joe or Meg. Or a lawyer. A cop.

Gripping the phone, she took a steadying breath. She'd already called him in panic once and didn't want to upset him further. But he needed to know.

"Rob," she stated, her voice surprisingly firm. In control now that she had a plan. "I have reason to believe Angie's mother is in town. I'm going to try to find her. Enlist her help. I'll call you when I know more. Bye."

Hurrying over to Angie, she lifted the child from the playpen and in no time readied her to go. Got her into shoes and a jacket. Dare she take Angie with her? Or should she leave her with Brett in the Singing Rock office?

But Rob said not to let her out of her sight.

Heading down the apartment stairs with Angie in her arms, a sudden thought struck her. What if she *did* find Cassie and convinced her to tell the truth to the officials? Could persuade her to come to Singing Rock and back Rob up in opposition to her parents?

Gut-kicked, she slowed her steps as she neared the door leading to the lodge's front porch. Reconnecting Cassie to daughter and daddy could stir up old feelings, couldn't it? Reignite romantic embers.

She could lose Rob. And Angie.

Dare she risk it?

Looking down at the solemn-eyed child gazing

up at her with eyes so like her father's, she could see only one answer.

Please, God, let me find Cassie.

Chapter Twenty

Over halfway home, Rob finished his calls and tossed the cell phone to the seat beside him. Then he pulled out onto the road again. The signal had faded in and out as he wound his way back into the high country, making the much-needed conversations difficult. He'd lost the signal altogether when he tried again to leave a message for Cassie. He wasn't one to drive and chat, but hadn't dared delay his departure from the Valley.

Angie and Olivia needed him.

Thanks to his brother-in-law, he'd secured a local lawyer, just in case—Jake Talford, one of the city councilmen. He'd filled the attorney in on the situation and he, in turn, intended to contact local law enforcement. Take a proactive step to ward off Cassie's parents.

Rob's hands tightened on the steering wheel as he glanced at the speedometer. Reluctantly he eased up on the gas. He'd promised Olivia he'd drive carefully. That he wouldn't go sailing off down a steep incline and into a rugged arroyo. He'd done all he could from a distance. Now he needed to get himself safely home.

Would he be required by law to give Cassie's parents shared custody? Visitation rights? He didn't want to deprive grandparents of a grandchild, but releasing Angie to these strangers who'd all but crippled the good-hearted Cassie sickened him. Jake said they'd approached out of the blue, with no advance communication, and had lied in an attempt to get Olivia to turn Angie over to them. So he could likely restrict contact to supervised visitation.

Cassie would back him up, wouldn't she? And Olivia? She'd been so insistent about him finding Cassie. Almost as though she herself needed confirmation that what he'd told her was the truth. That didn't sound like a woman who believed in him, one who was on his side, but rather one who didn't yet fully trust him. Had doubts. Was ready to bolt.

He glanced down at the phone on the seat next to him. He'd better pull over again and check for messages that may have come in while he'd been taking care of business. Maybe Olivia had called. Moments later he again tossed the phone aside. The message wasn't one he wanted to hear.

Cassie was in town. *Why?*

And Olivia intended to find her.

* * *

This wasn't the biggest town on the planet. But driving up and down the streets of Canyon Springs—surging with visitors intent on catching a glimpse of autumn color and end-of-season sales—Olivia still hadn't spotted Cassie's car. Two hours ago she'd glimpsed the rental belonging to Cassie's parents parked at one of the restaurants. Unfortunately, she wasn't gifted at distinguishing makes and models of cars. She only recalled that Cassie's was white—like almost every other car in Arizona.

Had she left town? Surely not, with her parents still here. But what was she up to? Why didn't she accompany her parents to Singing Rock to claim their grandchild? And why did she approach Olivia and Angie at the park? What was the point of that? Was she scouting things out so she could snatch Angie and run, as her parents claimed Rob had done?

Olivia glanced into the rearview mirror at the little girl buckled into her car seat and chewing on an animal cracker. A child innocently oblivious of the drama surrounding her. She glanced at the dashboard clock. Why hadn't Rob returned her call? He could be home by now, couldn't he? Not wanting to give up her search for Cassie, she nevertheless pulled her car into a motel lot and parked. Rolled down the window a few inches. Dug out her cell phone.

Phooey.

She'd accidentally turned off the ringer. Had messages waiting. All were from Rob. She punched in his number and he picked up.

"I'm home. Where are you?"

"I'm in town—with Angie. I didn't find Cassie."

"What made you think you recognized her in the first place? You've never even met her."

"I found a photo this morning." She held her breath, knowing it would take him two seconds to realize the only place she could have found it. "Then I knew I'd spoken with her yesterday."

"So she really is here."

"I'm sorry I couldn't find her, Rob."

"Just as well. Keep Angie with you. Don't come back to Singing Rock. Cassie's folks could show up any time. I need to get this straightened out."

The phone went dead in her unsteady hand.

How could she pray anything less than for the broken family to be reunited? She *had* to find Angie's mother.

"Libbia!"

"Yes, sweetie?"

"I'm thirsty."

With a heavy heart, she stowed the cell phone and reached for the carrying bag to retrieve a sippy cup of water. Handed the plastic container to the sleepy-eyed toddler.

"Tank you."

"You're—"

Olivia's heart stilled as her eyes focused outside

the window on a woman exiting from one of the motel rooms. *Cassie.* Heading right toward her. Or so it seemed for a second. Then she veered to a white car parked a couple of empty slots over from Olivia's. In an instant, she unbuckled her seatbelt and opened her own car door. Got out.

"Cassie?"

Startled, the woman glanced her way. But from the look on her face, she recognized Olivia at once.

"I need to talk to you." Olivia's voice came surprisingly firm. In control. Not to be denied.

The blonde met her halfway between the cars. The two women assessed each other in silence, Olivia reading uncertainty in the eyes of Angie's mother. What did she see reflected in Olivia's face? Curiosity? Fear? Determination?

"You're Cassie Wells, aren't you? The birth mother of Rob McGuire's daughter."

"I am."

"What are you doing here?"

A delicate eyebrow rose. No doubt she hadn't expected such a direct question, the harsh tone, but Olivia didn't have time to waste.

"I wanted to see her. See where she and Rob are living."

"You're having second thoughts about giving her up."

"No. Not at all," the woman stated firmly. "I'm assured, seeing this beautiful town. Seeing how she's being cared for. Knowing the sacrifices Rob's made and will continue to make on her behalf. Leaving her with him was the right thing to do."

Olivia scoffed. "Don't pretend. I know you're here with your parents. Here to claim Angie."

Her face paled. "My parents? What are you—"

"Why are you trying to harm Rob? Lying that he threatened you, kidnapped his daughter."

"Rob didn't—"

"That's what your parents are saying. I don't know what you're up to, but it's not going to work. Rob still has that note you left him when you took off. *Abandoned* Angie. I imagine he's saved your phone messages, too."

"Wait." Cassie held up her hand. "I'm not here to take her away from him. My parents are here? Right now?"

"To claim Angie on your behalf."

"You have to believe me, I had no idea."

Could she be telling the truth? Could her presence in Canyon Springs be a freak coincidence? She had, after all, called Rob to warn him, hadn't she?

"When I talked to them, they threatened to bring the law down on him. They're saying he forced you to give up your child."

"He didn't. It was my decision and I stand by it." She made a helpless motion. "This is all my fault. I never intended that my parents know about her. I got in a fight with them and—"

"That doesn't matter now. What matters is that the truth comes out. That you back up Rob. You'll do that, won't you?"

Cassie turned a wondering gaze in Angie's direction, her words coming softly. "I think that's why I'm here."

Olivia's scalp prickled, the sensation spreading down her arms. "What do you mean?"

"For the past week I've felt a strong impression that I should come here. To make sure all was well. I kept putting it off. I didn't want to see Rob or his daughter. But I finally gave in."

Olivia took a quivering breath. *Thank You, Lord.*

"Then come with me to Singing Rock, Cassie. Now."

Usually Rob stepped out on the shaded, wood-floored expanse of the lodge to welcome visitors, to offer his hand, hospitality and a smile. But not today.

"Mr. Wells?"

The man's eyes narrowed. "Robert McGuire?"

"I am."

"I should flatten you for what you did to my daughter." He lifted his chin pugnaciously, but the woman beside him—Cassie's stepmom?—placed a restraining hand on his arm.

How ironic that this pair should come to the defense of Cassie's honor when, from what he'd gleaned from her, they hadn't cared much about what she did or where she went once she was of an age when they no longer controlled the funds left by her mother.

"I won't deny a relationship with Cassie that brought our child into the world. But we both know I didn't kidnap my daughter as I've heard you've been proclaiming. So let's drop that tactic of yours right now. It's wasted on me. And won't hold up in a court of law."

Or at least it wouldn't if Cassie backed him up.

The man glanced toward the lodge's main door. "So where is she? My grandchild?"

"She's not on the property at the moment. I suggest you rethink whatever it is you have planned and go back to wherever you came from."

"We won't be dismissed so easily, Mr. McGuire. We intend to seek custody of our grandchild."

"That won't happen."

"Cassie wasn't in any condition to be making decisions about the welfare of her baby so soon after the birth," the woman inserted. "That post-partum syndrome, I imagine. Then you pressured her to—"

"No one pressured anyone to do anything. Cassie left of her own free will. She could have stayed. Been a mother to our daughter. Become my wife."

"And let you get your hands on her inheritance?"

"I cared nothing about that and she knew it. But it seems you had quite the interest in it at one time— and may have an interest in what your granddaughter may inherit from her maternal great-grandmother when the time comes."

"Don't fight us on this, McGuire. You'll wish you hadn't. We'll use any legal means at our disposal. Cassie will be discredited. A psychiatrist will prove my daughter was in no mental or emotional condition to make decisions about—"

"Dad."

The threesome spun toward the soft voice as a woman stepped out from the side of the building.

Cassie. And Olivia, with his sleeping daughter in her arms. He'd been so focused on these people intruding into his life, he hadn't noticed them pulling into the clearing.

Angie's mother had changed little since the last time he'd seen her. Since the night before she composed her note, taped it to the door of a bedroom they didn't share and drove off without waking him.

She stepped up on the porch, her signature flowing skirt wafting around her ankles. Her usually vibrant features hard with determination. "Don't do this, Dad."

Her father took a step toward her, then stopped, her body language holding him at bay. "We're here to help you, honey. Help you get your baby back."

"I don't want my baby back."

While the conviction in her voice brought Rob relief, the harshness of her words renewed sorrow for Angie's sake.

"This man took advantage of you, sweetheart. Then tricked you into giving up your child."

"Nobody tricked me. I stand by my decision." Her forehead puckered as she stared at him in disbelief. "Do you think I'd risk raising a child after the way you raised me? I don't know anything about healthy parenting. Or sustaining an adult relationship for that matter. All I ever saw or heard from you and Mom were arguments. Hateful, selfish encounters. You bullying, undermining Mom's self-esteem. And Mom retaliating passive-aggressively. That's no way to bring up a child. I will never allow my daughter to grow up in an environment like that."

"Now, Cassie—"

"You won't win, Dad. Not even with every single lawyer in the country at your disposal. I've confessed everything to Mom's mother, and Grandma has the means to tie this up in court until her great-grandchild is twenty-one if that's what it takes. You will not get your hands on this little girl."

"Hold on now—"

"Dad, for once in your life, listen to what I'm saying. Respect my wishes. I want this sweet child to grow up in a loving home like Rob can provide."

He cut Rob a belittling look. "A single man?"

"Yes, a single man." She glanced at Rob with a confident nod, then turned again to her father, eyes softening. Pleading. "Dad, in spite of everything in our past, I still care for you. Please don't do something to change that."

He stared at her for a long moment, a clash of emotions warring in his eyes, then he glanced at his wife.

She shook her head. "You're making a mistake, Cassandra."

"I've never been more sure of anything in my life."

Eyes still dark with anger and resentment, her father motioned to Angie. "Could I at least hold my grandchild?"

Rob stiffened, but Cassie was not to be swayed. "Not today, Dad. I imagine Rob will be willing to discuss supervised visitation if you think you still want that. I seriously doubt you will. There's nothing for you to gain from it."

Her father shot Rob a dirty look. Then he took his wife by the arm and returned to their car, making no effort to approach his daughter. To utter words of love and acceptance in spite of her own confession that she still cared for him. Was it any wonder Cassie couldn't grasp the concept of a Heavenly Father considering the example she'd had on earth?

"Daddy!" Still secured in Olivia's embrace, a sleepy-eyed Angie stretched her little arms out toward him. "Daddy!"

He strode to her and picked her up, letting his gaze speak his thankfulness to Olivia. But his heart ached. If only she'd believed him, had taken his word. Hadn't needed Cass to confirm the truthfulness of what he'd told her.

She looked away, almost as if ashamed, and he turned his attention to Angie's mother.

Chapter Twenty-One

Olivia could endure only a fleeting moment of watching from the sidelines as the threesome reunited. Seeing Cassie hold out a tentative hand to the little girl. Watching Angie clutch one of her fingers. Hearing Rob whisper, "Thank you, Cass. I can never thank you enough."

Biting back a sob, Olivia disappeared around the side of the lodge. Mother. Father. Daughter. It didn't come as a surprise. She'd known all along that bringing them together could cost her everything she held dear. And although Cassie said she didn't want her baby, that had only been a confession to divert her father from his intent. A means of throwing her support behind Rob. Presenting a united front.

She hadn't missed the thankfulness in Rob's eyes when he took Angie from her arms. Or the sadness. The regret. Of course he'd hate to hurt her. He had a kind and compassionate heart. But God was calling him to a different journey. One they didn't share.

Olivia all but stumbled beneath the towering ponderosas as she followed the winding, hard-packed dirt trail to the footbridge stretching over the creek. Even in her tumultuous teen years she'd always seemed to end up here. In this quiet place overlooking the tumbling waters.

Of course he'd choose the mother of his child. That was right. Good. The way God intended it to be. She didn't want to stand in the way of that. In the way of two hearts being healed. Of Angie having a family.

She took a ragged breath and rested her forearms on the bridge railing. Clenched her hands tight.

She couldn't stay here. Not with Rob managing Singing Rock, which he'd no doubt want to continue doing. He'd already come to love Canyon Springs. Believed God had led him here. Cassie would fall in love with it, too. And there was no more perfect place to raise Angie than this small town in the high country.

Staring up through the pine branches, she marveled at the brilliance of the blue sky overhead. Drank in the faint scent of the water, decaying vegetation, sun-warmed pine. Things she'd loved about Singing Rock since childhood. She thought she'd come home this time. For good. But it wasn't to be. She blinked back tears, determined not to give in to them.

Why'd her Heavenly Father always seem to bring her into relationships where her most important role

was to pray men she cared for through a difficult
time, to bring them back to a healthy relationship
with God, with others?

But she always ended up alone.

A jay called in the distance. Wind stirred in the
limbs overhead. The creek danced merrily among
the rocks, its sound soothing her battered soul.

I love you, and you can trust Me.

Tears again pricked her eyes, the gurgling waters
blurring. That's what God said every time her heart
was broken. When dreams were dashed. She wanted
to trust Him. Each time made every effort to trust
Him. Could she do it again?

"And that's the only reason I can give you for
coming to Canyon Springs," Cassie concluded. "Your
God wanted me here. Today. At this hour."

"He's your God, too, Cassie."

She shook her head. "I'm not there yet, Rob."

"God won't force Himself on you. But don't wait
too long to let Him in. You never know what tomorrow might bring."

She took a deep breath, dismissing his comment.
"I want you to understand nothing's changed. It's not
that I don't care for our daughter. I just don't—"

"Love her? Love isn't only a feeling, Cass. It's a
choice, too. A decision."

"I know it's hard for you to understand, but maybe
in a way I'm doing this because I *do* love her. The

two of you deserve nothing less than a woman who will make a choice to love you wholeheartedly. One who shares your beliefs about God. Who will commit to you. Partner with you. Grow happily old with you."

"Cass—"

"You know I'm not that person. Never was. But I believe there's someone in your life who is."

His mind flashed to where his heart dwelled. "Olivia."

She nodded. "She loves you, Rob. I'm sure of it."

He drew a weary breath. "How can she love a man she can't trust?"

"What makes you think she doesn't trust you?"

"When your parents spouted off ugly lies about me, she doubted what I'd told her about how I came to have Angie. Insisted that I find you, as if only you could be believed. Not me."

Cassie glared at him in exasperation. "For such a bright guy, you're so wrong. When she found me, she accused me of lying to my parents. Demanded to know why I'd want to harm you. Demanded that I set things straight. I saw no evidence that she thought there might be a truth contrary to what you'd told her."

His heart lightened. A little.

"You're not saying this, are you, to justify yourself, to give you an excuse to walk away from Angie again?"

"Gus is waiting for me and that, for now, is where I

belong. He's older. Has grown kids and doesn't want any more. I can contribute to his happiness, his well-being, in ways I would never be able to do for you or your daughter."

Her words rang true. Cassie would never make that kind of commitment to him. To Angie. He'd known that from the beginning.

They stood staring at each other. Two strangers. No more than the shallowest of acquaintances. Their only common bond held securely in his arms.

Heart heavy, he looked at the now-dozing Angie. "So what do I tell *her?* Do you want a part in her life? Of any kind?"

Cassie glanced away, as if she already knew he wouldn't like what she had to say. "I don't want her forming fantasies about her absentee birth mother. I can't parent her, not even from a distance."

"Cassie—"

"As she grows older, if she wants to contact me, wants to see me, I'm open to that. But she'll get hurt, Rob. I *will* hurt her, however unintentionally. That's why she needs you—and Olivia. A real dad. A real mom."

She gave Angie's tiny hand a gentle squeeze, then stepped back. "Look, I've got to get going. Already told Gus to start packing so we can leave as soon as I get back."

"Cass—"

"Let it go, Rob." Her gentle smile encouraged.

"Your God has blessed you with a beautiful little girl in spite of our shortcomings. Be thankful for that if for nothing else."

"I thank Him for Angie every single day. And I won't stop praying you'll come to know Him in a personal way, too."

"Who knows?" She shrugged, the corners of her mouth lifting. "You know I never say never."

"Don't be flippant about this, Cass."

"Then I wouldn't be me, now would I?"

She spun away as without a care in the world, her skirt swirling, then trotted down the porch steps.

"There's someone in your life who is."

If only that were true.

He watched as Cassie rounded the corner of the lodge. Heard her car start up. Saw her drive away. *Now what, Lord?*

"Daddy?" Angie rubbed at her eyes, trying to wake up.

"Yeah, sweetie?"

"Where's Libbia?"

"Do you want me to find her?"

She nodded.

"Then let's see if you can stay with Brett while I find her. Okay?"

"'kay."

Moments later, when he deposited Angie in the arms of the surprised cowboy, he promised an explanation later. From the grab Angie made at his Western hat, they'd be buddies in no time.

He hadn't heard Olivia's car start up, hadn't seen it pull out. Hadn't seen her walk over to her folks' place across the way. She had to be nearby. Maybe down by the creek, a place she'd once told him was one of her favorite retreats.

He eagerly hurried in that direction, down the trail and through the trees. But as he neared, heard the rush of water, his footsteps slowed.

They were to have had dinner together tonight at her request. He'd planned to tell her he loved her. Fill her arms with roses and promise her his heart. But now? What would he say when he found her? Dare he speak words of love? Would she tell him that meeting Cassie, an in-the-flesh reminder of the onetime relationship that brought Angie into the world, had changed things between them?

He couldn't blame her.

He'd let her down. She deserved better.

How can you expect God to bless your future if you won't turn loose of your past?

Her words echoed through his mind, mingling with the sweet sound of birdsong and the waters of the nearby creek. He drew in a steadying breath as he glimpsed her between the trees, through the autumn-bright underbrush. Standing on the footbridge, arms folded on the railing, she stared down at the water.

She'd gotten on his case about not accepting God's

gift of forgiveness. Intimated that he was implying God was a liar. She'd been right. Instead of reaching out an open hand to receive what God offered, for years he'd clenched it tight. Felt somehow—some way—that over time he'd be able to make up for his poor choices. Earn forgiveness. Finally feel he deserved it.

But forgiveness was a gift accepted through faith. Not a faith that earned it, but a faith that received it.

He couldn't earn Olivia's forgiveness, either. Would never be worthy of it. But would she give it to him freely even after coming face-to-face with the partner with whom he'd brought Angie into the world?

"Rob?"

She'd spied him. Was looking directly at him. Despite a gentle smile, she appeared troubled. Resigned. One look told him that what she had to say to him wouldn't be what he'd clung to in those flashing moments of hope. Forgiveness didn't mean there wouldn't be consequences for his wrong choices.

He slowly made his way down to the bridge, crunching the layered brown pine needles under his trudging feet. Footfalls echoing hollowly on the wooden slats, he joined her at the railing midway across the bridge.

"I'd hoped things would turn out differently," she blurted before he could bring himself to speak. "But having met Cassie..."

"I'm sorry, Olivia. So very sorry."

She didn't look at him. "Please don't apologize. I knew this could happen when I went looking for her. But I had to risk it, Rob. I hope you can understand that."

"Unfortunately, I do." He gripped the railing, willing himself to keep his tumbling emotions in check. Keep himself from gathering her into his arms and begging her to reconsider.

What were her plans now? As much as he believed God had led him here, as much as he wanted to raise Angie in Canyon Springs, he'd relinquish Singing Rock's management to Olivia. Move on. That's the least he could do.

"Looks like I'll be seeing the Holy Land soon," she said quietly. "I've always dreamed of that."

"You don't have to leave because of me. This is your home—and your opportunity to run the property."

"No. My folks will want to keep you in that role. I'm certain of that. Canyon Springs is an ideal setting for your fresh start. To form a real family with Angie—and Cassie."

He frowned. Had he missed something here?

"Cassie's not a part of the equation, Olivia. I thought I'd been clear about that from the beginning. I thought you understood."

"But I thought—I thought you'd come down here to—" She stared at him in confusion.

Had she thought he'd searched her out to tell her he and Cassie were now a couple? He tamped down the hope stirring in his heart. Even without Cassie in the picture, Olivia's own feelings toward him may have altered after encountering the woman from his past.

"As expected, she waved goodbye and hit the road."

"So the two of you, you're not—?"

"Nothing's changed between Cassie and me. She has someone else in her life. Wants no part of me. Wants little to do with Angie."

Dare he say it? Lay it out for her to accept—or reject?

"Olivia…" He reached for her hand. Her soft, gentle hand. His thumb brushed against it as he gazed at her, his every hope and dream no doubt laid bare in his eyes. "My heart, my life, are still available—if yours is."

A look of hesitant wonder filled her dark eyes.

"I love you, Olivia."

Her soft gasp signaled surprise—but not opposition. Encouraged, he reached for her other hand, as well. "I think you've come to care for me, too. But I'll understand if, because of my past, you can't return that love."

He braced himself as a trembling smile formed on her lips.

"Oh, but I do."

He stared, dumbfounded. "You do?"

Her grasp tightened on his hands. "I love you, Rob McGuire. I think I've loved you ever since we were in college."

"But I'm not the man you thought I was then. I blew it, Olivia. Big-time."

She tugged him closer, desperation to be understood reflecting in her eyes. "Don't you see, Rob? I'm no longer in love with a figment of my imagination. I love the you that you are now. Today. This very minute."

Could that be true?

"The man I am today?" A smiled tugged as he pulled a hand free to cup her sweet face. Searched the depths of her eyes. "A man complete with emotional scars and bruises and ugly stitch marks?"

"The whole package."

She loved him. Not the man she once thought he was. But *him*. A fierce joy pounded through his veins. He started to scoop her into his arms when a thought struck him. He grimaced.

Her eyes flickered. "What?"

"The roses." He let out an exasperated puff of breath. "They're in the refrigerator."

She looked at him in bewilderment. "What are you talking about?"

"Roses. And I was supposed to—" he chuckled and motioned to his work boots and jeans "—clean up. Dress up. I bought a dozen red roses. For tonight. For when I did this."

Dropping to one knee before an astonished Olivia, he gazed into her beautiful face.

"I love you with all my heart. And I thank God for creating you and bringing you into my life." He drew in a strengthening breath. "I don't have a ring yet. My sisters will kill me. But will you do me the honor of becoming my wife?"

For a long moment she stared at him, eyes filled with disbelief. Maybe he'd sprung this on her too quickly? Should have let her get used to the "L" word first. Given her time to grow into the idea of what the next logical step might be.

"Or maybe do me the honor—" he added quickly "—of thinking about it? Praying about it?"

A radiance filled her eyes. Laughter bubbled. "Oh, you big silly! Of course I'll marry you. I will! I will!"

She squealed. Did an in-place happy dance—so typical of Olivia—then pulled him to his feet. Fell into his arms...as if she'd always belonged there.

Epilogue

"A December wedding? Are you kidding me?" Reyna let out a yelp that echoed through the sanctuary of Canyon Springs Christian Church as the last of the congregation filed out following Sunday's service. She looped her arm through that of her bearded husband. "Is there a conspiracy to keep me from seeing my pastor hubby that whole month?"

"It's economical," Paulette said, nodding with a smiling approval that warmed Olivia's heart. "The church will be decorated for the season, right? Tree. Poinsettias. Twinkle lights. I think they're showing common sense."

"Wow. I hadn't thought of that." With a laugh, Olivia slipped her arm around Rob's waist, gazing into his smiling eyes in wonder. Astonished that God had transformed her college dream guy into a flesh-and-blood man who loved her. Who wanted to *marry* her.

"Cost-effectiveness? Whatever happened to romance?" Reyna shook her head sadly. "That must be what Trey and Kara are thinking, too. And Sandi and Bryce. I didn't know we had so many cheapos in our midst."

"Not cheapos," their oldest sister admonished. "Good stewards."

Olivia's father, standing behind her beaming mother, leaned around his wife, his low voice a stage whisper. "And as one who's played the traditional role of father of the bride—already footing the bill for three of the five—I don't want it getting around town that I put that idea in her head."

The extended Diaz family joined in the laughter. It was great to have Mom and Dad back. To see Brandi by her own mother's side, body language relaxed and reflecting the acceptance tentatively growing between them.

Rob took Olivia's hand. "Ready to pick up Angie? Hate to keep the Sunday School teachers waiting. We need to let them get home to their own families."

She gazed around the auditorium of the stone building, envisioning a winter evening a few months from now. Soft candlelight. Christmas hymns. Snow flurries dancing outside the windows. Herself in a simple white gown. Rob—and Angie—at her side. She squeezed her fiancé's strong hand and smiled up at him. "Ready when you are."

Side by side they headed under the covered walk-way to the adjacent classroom building.

"Mom and Dad are looking good, aren't they? So relaxed. And that's because of you, Rob. They'd never taken an extended time off like that before. Never would have done it if they hadn't put enormous trust in you."

"I think they were taken aback last night when they got home and heard our news."

"You think so?"

"I mean, you weren't even here when they left. They hardly knew me. Had no idea we'd known each other in college. And then they walk in the door and it's 'Hi, Mom! Hi, Dad! We're gonna be a family.'"

"Think it blew them away?"

"I was shaking in my boots most of the night. Knew it was a matter of time before your Dad hauled me out back and knocked me upside the head. Sent me packing with orders to keep away from his baby girl."

"Really?" Olivia laughed. "No way. They love you and adore Angie. I thought I'd never get Dad to turn her loose so I could get her put to bed. And Mom was every bit as bad."

"She was, wasn't she?" Rob grinned.

"And they're thrilled with the ideas we have for Singing Rock. That we'll be managing it together, like they did. Like Mom's parents did before them."

"I am grateful you didn't let me suggest a gourmet

coffee shop. Or an Olympic-size pool. That might have cast a shadow over their enthusiasm for a new son-in-law."

"Doubtful. They're so thrilled with you, I think you could have suggested a Disney-size roller coaster looping back and forth across the creek and they wouldn't have batted an eye." She drew him to an abrupt halt. Glanced mischievously in both directions of the empty hallway. "Kiss me."

"Here?" He drew back. Also glanced both ways. Then toward the heavens. "In front of God and everybody?"

"An itsy-bitsy one? To tide me over until after lunch?"

He groaned. "You're not going to make my life easy for the next couple of months, are you?"

"I have every confidence you'll survive." She lifted her head and closed her eyes in giddy expectation.

And much to her delight, she was duly rewarded.

"See?" A female voice carried down the empty hall. "They didn't forget you. There's your mommy and daddy!"

They broke apart and whirled in the direction of the nursery where a teenager stood, Angie in her arms. Both waving.

A quick glance confirmed Rob's ears reddening, but Olivia hurried down the hall, barely making it to the door before Angie made a lunge for her.

"Mommy!"

Mommy? Overcome by the endearment, she gathered the two-year-old into her arms. Cradled her warmth. Drew in her baby shampoo scent. Yes, Mommy. Not by a body's birth, but by a birth of the heart.

"Mommy. Kinda like the sound of that." Rob, now at her side, tugged playfully on the eyelet trim of Angie's dress, but his eyes were on Olivia. "Mommy. Wife. Nice combination for a beautiful woman."

The teen gave him an *oh, puleeze* look, then gathered her things, squeezed out the door and dashed down the hall.

Rob cocked a brow. "Think we embarrassed her?"

"Not likely. That's Cate Landreth's daughter. So expect it to be common knowledge by tomorrow that we were caught playing kissy face in the church's education wing."

"Kissy face, huh?" A smile tugged as he moved in a step closer, an impish light dancing in his eyes. "Well, then, Miz almost-McGuire, what do you say we give them something to talk about?"

Stick in the mud? Stuffy? Wasn't that what this man's sister once called him?

With a disbelieving laugh, she lifted her face to his.

Life was good. And getting better by the minute.

* * * * *

Dear Reader,

Welcome back to Canyon Springs! This "high country" region of Arizona is filled with beautiful little mountain communities featuring abundant campsites and cabin resorts like Singing Rock. It's a perfect spot for a getaway—to step back, quiet down and listen to the "still small voice" of God.

Rob McGuire came to Canyon Springs for a fresh start, but he faced many challenges of his own making. Sometimes our wrong choices go unnoticed by others. We ask for forgiveness and keep them "just between us and God." However, as in Rob's case, some choices may have more public and long-lasting consequences. They can create obstacles—including fear of rejection—in our relationship with God and with others.

I hope you've enjoyed Olivia and Rob's journey to recognizing God's loving mercy. Mercy evidenced through His forgiveness—not rejection—and bringing about good from decisions that fell far short of His own ideals.

I love to hear from readers, so please contact me via email at glynna@glynnakaye.com or Love Inspired Books, 233 Broadway, Suite 1001, New York, NY 10279. Please also visit my website at www.glynnakaye.com—and stop in at www.loveinspiredauthors.comandwww.seekerville.net.

Thank you for again joining me in Canyon Springs!
Glynna

Questions for Discussion

1. Rob's been in several relationships where he's faced personal rejection. How does that affect his relationship with Olivia?

2. How do you feel about Rob's initial relationship with his daughter's mother? His relationship with her now? How would you feel if you were in Rob's shoes?

3. Several years ago Rob did not uphold his personal beliefs and allowed his relationship with God to erode. Have you ever experienced "spiritual erosion"? How did that come about? What were the consequences?

4. While Rob knows God forgave him when he first asked, he still has trouble accepting that forgiveness because he doesn't believe he deserves it. Why is that?

5. How does Olivia's "placing Rob on a pedestal" make confessing his past more difficult? Do we ever want to be accepted just as we are, with all our flaws and failures, yet withhold that same freedom from others? How can we see both ourselves and others more realistically and allow God to take care of the imperfections?

6. Olivia went through Rob's personal belongings—including a locked file box—in a desperate search for a phone number. Rob didn't seem to mind, but do you think her actions were justified? Would you have done the same?

7. Olivia feels misunderstood by her family, especially her oldest sister. She wants to find her "purpose" in life, so she tries new things to see if God will open or close doors. Have you ever had a time in your life when you tried something new to confirm if it was God's plan for you? Did He open or close doors?

8. Do you agree with Meg's assessment that the fear of rejection can lead to self-imposed isolation and superficial relationships? Have you ever had to risk rejection? How did it turn out?

9. Brandi is experiencing growing pains and not feeling accepted for who she is. She falls in with the wrong crowd. How influential was peer pressure when you were growing up? How much does it influence you now? How might Brandi's family have better helped her to stand strong against peer pressure?

10. Olivia is disappointed when she discovers Rob isn't the "perfect" man she'd thought he was in college. How are her eyes opened to recognizing

she loves the real man he is now more than she loved the dream she'd fallen for so many years ago?

11. After the near-miss situation in Las Vegas, Rob heads far away from the city lights. But he can't outrun his past. Have you ever "started fresh," only to discover you'd brought "you" along with you? Did God still confront you with the issues you were trying to escape? What was the outcome?

12. Romans 8:28 says "And we know that in all things God works for the good of those who love him." The scripture doesn't say all things are good, but that God works for our good in all things if we love Him. Have you ever experienced God turning something around to be a blessing to you or others that was clearly a wrong choice, not His preferred choice?

LARGER-PRINT BOOKS!

**GET 2 FREE
LARGER-PRINT NOVELS
PLUS 2 FREE
MYSTERY GIFTS**

Larger-print novels are now available...

YES! Please send me 2 FREE LARGER-PRINT Love Inspired® novels and my 2 FREE mystery gifts (gifts are worth about $10). After receiving them, if I don't wish to receive any more books, I can return the shipping statement marked "cancel". If I don't cancel, I will receive 6 brand-new novels every month and be billed just $4.99 per book in the U.S. or $5.49 per book in Canada. That's a saving of at least 23% off the cover price. It's quite a bargain! Shipping and handling is just 50¢ per book in the U.S. and 75¢ per book in Canada.* I understand that accepting the 2 free books and gifts places me under no obligation to buy anything. I can always return a shipment and cancel at any time. Even if I never buy another book, the two free books and gifts are mine to keep forever.

122/322 IDN FEG3

Name _____ (PLEASE PRINT)

Address _____ Apt. #

City _____ State/Prov. _____ Zip/Postal Code

Signature (if under 18, a parent or guardian must sign)

Mail to the **Reader Service:**
IN U.S.A.: P.O. Box 1867, Buffalo, NY 14240-1867
IN CANADA: P.O. Box 609, Fort Erie, Ontario L2A 5X3

Not valid to current subscribers to Love Inspired Larger-Print books.

**Are you a current subscriber to Love Inspired books
and want to receive the larger-print edition?
Call 1-800-873-8635 or visit www.ReaderService.com.**

* Terms and prices subject to change without notice. Prices do not include applicable taxes. Sales tax applicable in N.Y. Canadian residents will be charged applicable taxes. Offer not valid in Quebec. This offer is limited to one order per household. All orders subject to credit approval. Credit or debit balances in a customer's account(s) may be offset by any other outstanding balance owed by or to the customer. Please allow 4 to 6 weeks for delivery. Offer available while quantities last.

Your Privacy—The Reader Service is committed to protecting your privacy. Our Privacy Policy is available online at www.ReaderService.com or upon request from the Reader Service.

We make a portion of our mailing list available to reputable third parties that offer products we believe may interest you. If you prefer that we not exchange your name with third parties, or if you wish to clarify or modify your communication preferences, please visit us at www.ReaderService.com/consumerschoice or write to us at Reader Service Preference Service, P.O. Box 9062, Buffalo, NY 14269. Include your complete name and address.

LILPI1B

Love Inspired®

SUSPENSE
RIVETING INSPIRATIONAL ROMANCE

Watch for our series of edge-
of-your-seat suspense novels.
These contemporary tales
of intrigue and romance
feature Christian characters
facing challenges to their faith...
and their lives!

AVAILABLE IN REGULAR
& LARGER-PRINT FORMATS